"He's in love with her!"

Mrs. Rodner sighed happily as Megan and her handsome professor waved goodbye.

Her husband took her arm. "Really? Has he told you so?" He sounded amused.

"Of course not. He won't tell anyone, certainly not our Meg, until he's good and ready."

"How do you know this, my dear?"

"He didn't even look at her when we came in, just nodded, but didn't you see the way he stared down at her as she got into the car?"

"Well, no, my dear, I can't say that I did, and if you're right, and I must say I find it unlikely, what about Meg's fiancé?"

"Oh, he fell in love with your *other* daughter weeks ago!"

Betty Neels is well-known for her romances set in the Netherlands, which is hardly surprising. She married a Dutchman and spent the first twelve years of their marriage living in Holland and working as a nurse. Today, she and her husband make their home in an ancient stone cottage in England's West Country, but they return to Holland often. She loves to explore tiny villages and tour privately owned homes there in order to lend an air of authenticity to the background of her books.

Books by Betty Neels

HARLEQUIN ROMANCE
3185—THE MOST MARVELLOUS SUMMER
3197—THE FINAL TOUCH
3208—A KIND OF MAGIC
3222—AN UNLIKELY ROMANCE
3249—ROMANTIC ENCOUNTER
3267—A HAPPY MEETING

Don't miss any of our special offers. Write to us at the following address for information on our newest releases.

Harlequin Reader Service
P.O. Box 1397, Buffalo, NY 14240
Canadian address: P.O. Box 603,
Fort Erie, Ont. L2A 5X3

THE QUIET PROFESSOR
Betty Neels

Harlequin Books

TORONTO • NEW YORK • LONDON
AMSTERDAM • PARIS • SYDNEY • HAMBURG
STOCKHOLM • ATHENS • TOKYO • MILAN
MADRID • WARSAW • BUDAPEST • AUCKLAND

Original hardcover edition published in 1992
by Mills & Boon Limited

ISBN 0-373-03279-X

Harlequin Romance first edition September 1993

THE QUIET PROFESSOR

CHAPTER ONE

THE corridor was gloomy by reason of its being on the top floor of the oldest part of the hospital, and largely unused save by the staff of the pathological department and anyone needing to visit them. One such visitor was standing there now, just where the corridor turned at a sharp angle, staring with horror at the shattered glass dish at her feet. She had been carrying it, and its grisly contents, and, believing there to be no one to impede her progress, had been running...

The person she had run into eyed the horrid mess on the floor thoughtfully. She was a tall, splendidly built girl, with dark hair twisted into an elegant chignon, a pretty face and large brown eyes.

She said calmly, 'You were running, Nurse Wells.' It wasn't an accusation, merely a statement. 'I take it that this is—was the specimen from Mrs Dodds? Do go and tell Professor van Belfeld that you have had an accident with it.'

Nurse Wells was a very junior nurse, healthily in awe of her seniors. She whispered, 'I daren't, Sister. He—he frightens me. When I dropped the forceps last week on the ward he looked at me. I know he didn't say anything but he—he just looked. Could I write him a note?'

Megan Rodner suppressed a smile. 'Well, no, I think not, Nurse.' She paused, looking at the woebegone face before her; any minute now and Nurse Wells was going to burst into a storm of tears. 'Go back to the ward, and tell Staff Nurse to give you something to do where

5

you can pull yourself together. I'll see Professor van Belfeld and explain.'

She was rewarded with a relieved sniff and a watery smile. 'Oh, Sister, you are a dear—I'll work ever so hard...'

'Good—and don't run!'

Left alone, Megan stood for a mere moment staring down at the ruined result of several days' treatment on Mrs Dodds, who hadn't been co-operative and would be even less so now. The professor would be annoyed, hiding icy anger behind a calm face. Unlike Nurse Wells, Megan wasn't afraid of him—she rather liked him, as far as one could like a person who made no effort to be more than coldly courteous.

She walked down a small dark passage leading off the corridor and opened the door at its end. The path. lab. was a complexity of several large rooms, all occupied by white-coated workers and a vast amount of equipment; she went past them all, exchanging hellos as she went, and tapped on a door in the last of the rooms.

The professor's room was quiet after the hum of noise from the rest of the department. He was sitting at his desk, writing, a big man with wide shoulders and fair hair thickly sprinkled with grey. He said without looking up, 'Yes?'

'Sister Rodner from Queen's Ward, sir. The specimen from Mrs Dodds——'

He interrupted her, 'Ah, yes, leave it with Peters; I'll need to see it myself.' He added belatedly, 'Thank you, Sister.'

'I haven't got it,' said Megan baldly. 'The dish was— that is, it's smashed.'

He looked up then, his cold blue eyes searching her face. She studied his face as she waited for him to say something. He was a handsome man with a commanding nose and a mouth which could become thin at times. It was thin now. 'Where is it?' His voice was quiet.

'In the corridor...'

He got up, towering over her. 'Come with me, Sister, and we will take a look.' He held the door and she went past him, back through the department and out into the corridor with him at her heels, and she stood silently while he crouched down to take a close look. He got to his feet and growled something she couldn't understand—Dutch swear words, she reflected, and she could hardly blame him. 'You dropped the dish, Sister?' His voice, with its faint accent, was gently enquiring.

She looked him in the eye. 'It fell, sir.'

'Just so. And whom are you shielding behind your—er—person, Sister?'

When she didn't answer, he said, 'You are perhaps afraid to tell me?'

'Good heavens, no,' said Megan cheerfully, 'I'm not in the least afraid of you, you know.'

He said nothing to that, only gave her a frigid stare. 'Be good enough to repeat the treatment, Sister, and when it is completed kindly let me know and I will send one of the technicians to your ward to collect it.'

She smiled at him. 'Very well, sir. I'm sorry about the accident; it's kind of you not to be too annoyed.'

'Annoyed? I am extremely angry,' he told her. 'Good day to you, Sister.'

Dismissed, she walked away and he watched her go, very neat in her dark blue uniform and the muslin trifle the sisters at Regent's wore upon their heads. Only when she had reached the end of the corridor and was out of sight did he go back to his office.

Megan went back to her ward, spent a difficult fifteen minutes persuading Mrs Dodds that it was necessary to repeat the treatment once again, and then repaired to her office to drink a soothing cup of tea and wrestle with the off-duty book. She was joined presently by her senior staff nurse, Jenny Morgan.

'Nurse Wells is in the linen cupboard, tidying. She's still crying.'

'Are there enough of us on to keep her there for a bit? The list will be starting soon—you'd better take the first case up. Nurse Craig can take the next one...' She plotted out the afternoon's work and Jenny poured second cups.

'Was he furious?' she wanted to know.

'Yes, but very polite. He'll send a technician when the next specimen's ready.'

'Oh, good. No one knows anything about him, do they? Perhaps he's crossed in love.' Jenny, who was for ever falling in and out of love with various housemen, sounded sympathetic.

Megan had opened the off-duty book again, and she said indifferently, 'I dare say the man's married with half a dozen children. He might be quite nice at home.'

Jenny went away and she concentrated on the off duty, but not for long. She was going out that evening, a rather special occasion, for she was to meet Oscar's parents. She had been engaged to Oscar for six months now and this was the first time she was to meet his family. He was a medical registrar, considered to be an up-and-coming young man with a good future. He had singled her out a year or more ago and in due course he had proposed. She had had her twenty-eighth birthday a day or two before that and since he seemed devoted to her and she liked him very much, indeed was half in love with him, she had agreed to become engaged. She had had proposals before but somehow she had refused them all, aware that deep inside her was a special wish to meet a man who would sweep her off her feet and leave her in no doubt that life without him would be of no use at all, but in her sensible moments she knew that she expected too much out of life. Solid affection, a liking for the same things—those were the things which made a successful marriage. In due course, she supposed, she would become Mrs Oscar Fielding. During their engagement she had endeavoured to model herself on Oscar's ideas of womanhood; he had hinted that she was a little too extravagant—what need had she to buy so many clothes when she spent so much of her time in uniform? And shoes—did she really need to buy expensive Italian shoes? He was always very nice about it and she had done her best to please him but just once or twice lately she had wondered if she was living up to his ideals. He never allowed her to pay her share when they went out together nor had he suggested that she should save for their future, with the consequence that she had a nice little nest-egg burning a hole in her pocket. She would, she decided, have to talk to him about it. It wasn't as if she wasted her money—she bought good clothes; classical styles which didn't date, but just lately she hadn't bought anything at all, wishing to please him. Perhaps she would get the chance to talk to him that evening.

The theatre cases went up and came back, she applied herself to the running of the ward and at five o'clock handed over to Jenny.

'Going out, Sister?' asked Jenny, tidying away the report book.

'Yes, with Oscar—I'm meeting his people.'

'Have a lovely evening,' her right hand wished her. 'It's take-in tomorrow. I expect you'll go somewhere nice.'

She spoke sincerely. She liked Sister Rodner but she thought Oscar was a stuffed shirt. Not nearly good enough for the beautiful creature preparing to leave the office.

In her room, Megan inspected her wardrobe. Something suitable, but what was suitable for meeting one's future in-laws? She decided upon a crêpe-de-Chine dress in a pleasing shade of azure blue, long-sleeved and high-necked, and covered it with a long loose coat in a darker blue. The coat was a very fine wool and had cost a lot of money justified by its elegance. She chose the plainest of her Italian shoes, found a handbag and gloves and went down to the hospital entrance.

He was waiting for her; he was also in deep conversation with Professor van Belfeld, who saw her first but gave no sign of having done so. Megan wasn't a girl to dither; she walked across to them and said, 'Good evening, sir' and then, 'Good evening, Oscar.'

The professor rumbled a good evening and Oscar said self-consciously, 'Oh, hello, Megan. Of course you know the professor?'

'Indeed, yes.' She gave him a smiling nod.

'Don't let me keep you,' said the professor. He sounded quite fatherly. 'I wish you a very pleasant evening.'

Oscar beamed at him. 'Oh, I'm sure of that, sir. Megan is to meet my parents for the first time.'

'Ah—delightful, I'm sure.' His chilly gaze took in the diamond ring on her finger, his face expressionless.

He watched them get into Oscar's elderly car before turning away and going to the wards.

Oscar's parents had come to London from their home in Essex. It was their habit to spend a few days each year at a modest hotel, attend a concert, see a suitable play and see as much of their son as possible. Megan, who had received a polite letter from his mother when they had got engaged, was feeling nervous. Supposing his mother and father didn't like her; supposing she didn't like them? She voiced her uncertainty to Oscar who laughed. 'Of course you'll like each other,' he told her. 'There's no reason why you shouldn't.'

Which was true enough. All the same, when they got to the hotel and joined the Fieldings in the half-empty bar she knew at once that she and Oscar's mother disliked each other at first glance. Not that there was any sign of this; they kissed the air beside each other's cheeks, said how glad they were to meet at last and made polite remarks about the splendid weather for March. There was a short respite while she was introduced to Oscar's father, a small man with a wispy moustache and an air of apology; she liked him but they had little chance to talk for Oscar seated them at a small table, ordered drinks and settled down to talk to his father.

Megan sipped the gin and tonic which she hadn't asked for and which she didn't like and engaged her future mother-in-law in small talk. Mrs Fielding brushed aside the chat and embarked on a cross-examination of Megan's life, her family, where had she gone to school, just how old she was... and it was to be hoped that she was a home-loving girl. 'These career-minded young women,' observed Mrs Fielding severely, 'have no right to go to work when they have a family and a husband to look after.'

Megan looked at her companion. She was short and stout with a sharp nose and beady eyes, dressed in what

Megan could only describe as economical clothes and
with a fearsome hair-do. Oscar had told her that they
were in comfortable circumstances and she had no reason
to doubt him; perhaps they were just careful of their
money... It seemed as though that was the case, for
when they sat down to dinner Mrs Fielding made it clear
that they would all have the set menu. 'I'm sure we shall
enjoy it,' she said in a voice daring anyone to say
otherwise, 'and a glass of wine is sufficient for us.'

It surprised her that Oscar did not seem to mind his
mother's managing ways; he affably agreed to everything she suggested and when she observed presently that
when they married they could have a quantity of furniture stored in the attics he thought it a splendid idea.

'What kind of furniture?' asked Megan.

'Oh, tables and chairs and a very large sideboard and
several carpets which I inherited from my parents. There
are several things from Mr Fielding's father too, I believe. Some quite nice chests of drawers, and, if I remember rightly, a pretty what-not.'

Megan, uncertain as to what a what-not might be, decided to say nothing. Later she and Oscar would have
a talk. When—a small voice added if—they married, she
wanted, like every other young woman, to choose her
own home. Where was that home going to be, anyway?
Somehow she and Oscar hadn't got around to talking
about that.

Later as they drove back to Regent's she asked. 'Oscar,
what do you plan to do when you've finished at
Regent's?'

'Get a senior post—I'd like to stay here but there might
not be an opening. Plenty of other hospitals in London,
though.'

'You want to stay here, in London, for always?'

'Possibly. I'll have to see what turns up.'

'What about me?'

'Well, if I can get a flat with the job I should think the best thing would be that; if not it would be best for you to live with Mother and Father. I could come home for weekends and free days—it's only a couple of hours in the car.'

'You don't mean that, do you?'

'Mean it? Of course I do. What else is there to do? It would be a waste of money to pay r a flat or even rooms when you can live at home for tl e price of your keep.' He laughed and patted her knee. 'If I thought you...but you're such a sensible girl...'

She glanced at him; he had a nice face, oper and good-natured. In a few years' time he would be a thoroughly reliable physician with a sound practice. He was fond of her too, although she sometimes thought that his work was his real love and he wasn't a man to sweep her off her feet. Sometimes she would have liked to have been swept...

He walked with her to the entrance to the nurses' home when they reached Regent's and stood for a moment, mulling over their evening.

'Take-in tomorrow,' said Megan.

'Shan't see much of you, though. When's your next weekend? I might be able to get Sunday off.'

'Could you? We could go home—you haven't met Mother and Father or the family yet. I'm free the weekend after next.'

'I'll see what I can do.' He kissed her without wasting much time over it. 'Sleep well, Megan. We might manage an hour or two during the week.'

'I'll do my best.'

She went to her room and presently, in bed, went over the evening. It hadn't been a huge success but she supposed that with time she and Oscar's mother might get to like each other. He should, she thought, sleepily, have fallen in love with a shy, quiet girl, content to take second place to his work and be suitably meek with his mother. She fell asleep trying to think of a way to turn herself into such a girl.

She discarded the idea the next morning. It was no good being meek and shy in her job; meekness would get her nowhere with the laundry superintendent who always argued about the excessive bedlinen Megan needed for her ward, nor would it help with the pharmacy, presided over by a bad-tempered man who queried every request and then said that he hadn't got it. She fought her way through a busy morning and went to her midday dinner with a sigh of relief, but as she swallowed the first mouthful of shepherd's pie she was recalled to the ward. Two street accidents; Eva Chambers, the senior casualty sister, gave her the details. 'You'll have your work cut out. I hope you have plenty of staff on duty.'

Head injuries, both of them, and so restless that Megan had to deplete her staff to special the two women. Mr Bright, one of the consultant surgeons, gave it his opinion that they needed to go to Theatre at once. 'Get them cross-matched, Sister,' he ordered, 'and checked for AIDS. Tell the path. lab. to send someone capable of dealing with them if they get too restless; they're both well-built women and there's a great deal of cerebral irritation.'

The path. lab. responded smartly. Megan, sailing down the ward to give a helping hand in answer to urgent sounds coming from behind the curtains, was overtaken by a soft-footed Professor van Belfeld. He said mildly, 'I understand that there is a certain amount of cerebral irritation—I thought it might be best if I came myself.'

'Oh, good,' said Megan. 'They're both a bit of a handful—we've got cot sides up, of course, but they will climb over...'

The professor had certainly been the right person to deal with the situation; he was gentle but he was also possessed of a strength which made child's play of re-straining the unconscious women. Megan, left to wrestle with arms and legs flying in all directions, watched him go and wished that he could have stayed.

Both women went to ICU after Theatre and the ward settled down to its normal routine; all the same it had been a busy day and she was glad to go off duty at last. Supper, a pot of tea, a hot bath and bed, she thought contentedly, going through the hospital; several long corridors, two staircases and the entrance hall to cross to reach the canteen in the basement. She had reached the hall when she saw the professor ahead of her. He was walking unhurriedly towards the doors. Going home, she supposed, and fell to wondering where home was. Why was he so late? Surely he didn't need to put in a twelve-hour day?

He turned round and saw her as she drew level with the entrance. 'A busy day, Sister Rodner,' he observed. 'Goodnight.'

She wished him goodnight too and as he went through the doors paused to watch him cross the forecourt and get into his car—a grey Rolls-Royce—and drive away. Just for a moment she found herself wishing that she could go with him and see where he lived...

Take-in went from Wednesday until Tuesday mid-night and was as busy as one might expect. Regent's was north of the river, its mid-Victorian bulk spread in the middle of streets packed with small houses, derelict buildings and small factories. There was always something, observed Eva Chambers wearily, at the end of a particularly busy day; if someone didn't damage themselves with factory machinery, they got run over by a car or stabbed by a member of a rival gang of youths. The weekend was always the worst; Megan, gloomily surveying her bulging ward, thanked heaven that Wednesday was in sight.

She had seen Oscar only once or twice and then only for a brief hour snatched in a grubby little café across the street from the hospital, but she went out in her off duty however tired she was. There was nowhere much to go, but a brisk walk made a nice change and the weather was kind; it was mild for the end of March and here and there was a gallant little tree or privet hedge in a rare front garden, and there were green shoots. Next week, she thought happily, she and Oscar would go home together, and the week after that she would have her own small flat; Theatre Sister was getting married and no longer needed the semi-basement she had lived in for some years, and Megan had jumped at the chance of getting it. Oscar hadn't liked the idea but, as she pointed out, it would be marvellous to have somewhere to go; she could cook supper and they could talk, something for which they seldom had time.

The ward settled back into its usual routine—admissions for operations, discharges for those who had recovered, dressings, treatment, serving meals, arranging the off-duty rota to please the nurses, continuing her running fight with the laundry; after four years she had become adept at running a ward.

Oscar wasn't free until Sunday and although she grudged missing a day at home it gave her the chance to go along to the flat and make her final arrangements for moving in. She had already met the landlord, an elderly bewhiskered cockney who occupied the ground-floor flat himself and let the top flat to a severe lady whose staid manner and ladylike ways added, he considered, to the tone of his house, something he was anxious to maintain in the rather shabby street.

Shabby or not, it was handy for the hospital, and Megan was looking forward to having a place of her own even if it was a down-at-heel semi-basement. She spent most of her Saturday going through its contents with Theatre Sister, who was packing up ready to leave, and she agreed to take over most of the simple furniture which was there and adopt the stray cat that went with the flat. It would be nice to have company in the evenings and he seemed an amiable beast. She went back to the hospital in the early evening, eager to make her move, noting with satisfaction that it took her exactly five minutes to get there. Her head full of pleasant plans about new curtains, a coat of paint on the depressing little front door, she failed to see Professor van Belfeld driving out of the forecourt as she went in.

She and Oscar left early the next morning. Her home in Buckinghamshire was in a small village north of the country town of Thame. Her father was senior partner in a firm of solicitors and had lived most of his life at Little Swanley, driving to and from his offices in Thame and Aylesbury. She had been born there, as had her younger sister and much younger brother, and although she enjoyed her job she was essentially a country girl. She had a small car and spent her free weekends and holidays at home, and she had hoped—indeed, half expected—that Oscar would get a partnership in a country practice; his determination to stay in London had shaken her a little. Sitting beside him as he drove out of London, she hoped that a day spent at her home would cause him to change his mind.

Little Swanley was a little over sixty miles' drive from Regent's and once they were out of the suburbs Oscar took the A41, and, when they reached Aylesbury, turned on to the Thame road before taking the narrow road leading to Little Swanley.

'It would have been quicker if we had taken the M40,' he pointed out as he slowed to let a farm cart pass.

'Yes, I know, but this is so much prettier—I don't like motorways, but we'll go back that way if you like.'

She felt a twinge of disappointment in his lack of interest in the countryside; after the drab streets round the hospital, the fields and hedges were green, there were primroses by the side of the road and the trees were showing their new leaves. Spring had come early.

Another even narrower road led downhill into the village. Megan, seeing the church tower beyond it, the gables of the manor house and the red tiles of the little cluster of houses around the market cross, felt a thrill of happiness. 'Go through the village,' she told Oscar. 'Ours is the first house on the left—there's a white gate...'

The gate was seldom closed. Oscar drove up the short drive and stopped before the open door of her home, white-walled and timber-framed with shutters at its windows, a roomy seventeenth-century house surrounded by trees with a lawn before it and flowerbeds packed with daffodils.

She turned a beaming face to Oscar. 'Home!' she cried. 'Come on in, Mother will be waiting.'

Her mother was already at the door, a still pretty woman almost as tall as her daughter. 'Darling, here you are at last, and you've brought Oscar with you.' She embraced Megan and shook hands with him. 'We've heard so much about you that we feel as though we know you already.' She opened the door wider. 'Come and meet my husband.'

Mr Rodner came into the hall then, the Sunday papers under one arm, spectacles on his nose, a good deal older than his wife, with a thick head of grey hair and a pleasant scholarly face. Megan hugged him before introducing Oscar. 'At last we've managed to get here together. Are the others home?'

'Church,' said her mother. 'They'll be here in half an hour or so; there's just time for us to have a cup of coffee and a chat before they get back.'

Melanie and Colin came in presently. Melanie was quite unlike her mother and sister; she was small and slim with golden hair and big blue eyes and Oscar couldn't take his eyes off her. Megan beamed on them both, delighted that they were instant friends, for Melanie was shy and gentle and tended to shelter behind her sister's Junoesque proportions. She left them talking happily and went into the garden to look at Colin's rabbits, lending a sympathetic ear to his schoolboy grumbles, then she went to help her mother put lunch on the table.

Oscar, she saw with happy relief, had made himself at home, and her parents liked him. She had thought they might have taken a walk after lunch and discussed their future but he was so obviously happy in their company that she gave up the idea and left him with her father, Colin and Melanie and she went into the kitchen to gossip with her mother while they cleared away the dishes and put things ready for tea.

'I like your young man,' said her mother, polishing her best glasses. 'He seems very sensible and steady. He'll make a good husband, darling.'

'Yes.' Megan hesitated. 'Only I don't see much chance of us marrying for a while—for a long while. He's rather keen on settling in London and I would have liked him to have found a country practice. I like my work, Mother, but I don't like London, at least not the part where we work.'

'Perhaps you can change his mind for him,' suggested Mrs Rodner comfortably. 'He doesn't want to specialise, does he?'

'No, but he's keen to get as many qualifications as he can and that means hospital posts for some time.'

'Did you like his parents, darling?'

Megan put down the last of the knives. 'Well, his father is quite nice—not a bit like Father, though. I tried hard to like his mother but she doesn't like me; she says she has no patience with career-minded girls.'

'You won't work once you are married, will you?'

'No. Oscar wouldn't like that. He thought it would be a good idea if he were to get a senior registrar's post at one of the big teaching hospitals and I were to live with his parents...'

'That won't work,' said Mrs Rodner with some heat. 'What would you do all day? And it wouldn't be a home of your own. Besides, after running a ward for a year or two you won't settle down easily to playing second fiddle to Oscar's mother, especially if you don't like her.'

'What shall I do?' asked Megan. 'It's a problem, isn't it?'

'Wait and see, darling. Very hard to do, I know, but it's the only way.'

Oscar drove her back to Regent's after supper, waiting patiently while she hugged and kissed her family in turn, cuddled the elderly Labrador, Janus, made a last inspection of the family cat, Candy, and her various kittens, and picked a bunch of daffodils to cheer up her room. He was seldom put out, she thought contentedly as she got into the car at last.

'Well,' she asked him as they drove away, 'did you like my family?'

'Very much. Your brother is pretty sharp, isn't he? Does well at school, I dare say.'

'Yes, and a good thing, for Father wants him to go into the firm later on.'

'Your sister is—she's charming, like a shy angel—you're not a bit alike,' and when Megan laughed at that he said, 'That sounds all wrong but you know what I mean. Has she got a job?'

'No, she helps Mother at home, but she's a marvellous needlewoman and she paints and draws and makes her own gloves—that kind of thing. She's a good cook too.'

'Those scones at tea were delicious,' said Oscar warmly. 'I like to think of her in the kitchen...'

Megan, faintly puzzled by this remark, refrained from telling him that she had knocked up a batch of scones while he had been talking to Melanie in the drawing-room. It was natural enough, she supposed, that he would think that being a ward sister precluded a knowledge of the art of cooking.

At the hospital they parted in the entrance hall.

'It was a delightful day,' said Oscar warmly. 'I haven't enjoyed myself so much for a long time.'

A remark which caused Megan to feel vaguely put out. All the same she said in her matter-of-fact way, 'Good, we must do it again. Don't forget I'm moving into my flat this week. If you're free on Thursday evening, you can come for supper.'

He kissed her cheek, since there was no one there to see. 'That's a date. What will it be? Baked beans on toast and instant coffee?'

She smiled. 'Very likely. You'd better bring a bottle of beer to help it out. Goodnight, Oscar.'

Before she went to sleep she had planned a supper menu which would put all thoughts of baked beans out of his head.

Theatre Sister left on Monday and on Tuesday evening Megan went round to the flat. She had already met the landlord and someone had been in to give the flat a good clean; it only remained for her to set the place to rights and since she had the evening before her she went back to the hospital, packed a case with most of her clothes, filled a plastic bag with books and went off once more. She had gone through the entrance door when the case was taken from her hand.

'Allow me,' said Professor van Belfeld. 'The car's over here...'

Megan stopped to look at him. 'Car?' she asked stupidly. 'But I'm only going——'

He interrupted her. 'To your new flat, no doubt. I'll drop you off as I go.'

'Well, that's very kind,' began Megan, 'but really there's no need.'

He didn't answer, but put a large hand under her elbow, took the bag of books away from her and steered her to his car. It was extremely comfortable sitting there beside him, only she didn't have time to enjoy it to the full; the journey took less than a minute.

Outside the shabby house he got out to open her door, took the key from her and unlocked the door of the flat, switching on the lights and then going back for her case and the books. The place looked bare and unlived-in but it was clean and needed only a few cushions, some flowers and photos and the small gas fire lighted. She was standing in the tiny lobby thanking the professor when the cat sped past them.

'Yours?' asked the professor.

'Well, yes. Theatre Sister said that she'd been feeding him. I'll get some milk, he must be hungry.'

A small group of children had collected round the car, staring in, and the professor turned round to look at them, picked out the biggest boy and beckoned him over. 'Go to the shop at the end of the street; I fancy it is still open. Buy two tins of cat food and some milk—any kind of milk.' He gave the lad some money. 'Fifty pence if you're quick about it.'

'Really,' protested Megan, 'there was no need...'

'The beast is hungry.' He stated the fact in his quiet voice, putting an end to further argument. 'You do not mean to stay here tonight?'

'No. I'm moving in tomorrow. I've a day off on Thursday and I'm going to cook a splendid supper. Oscar's coming.' She added, 'Dr Fielding.'

'Yes. I do know him,' said the Professor drily. He sounded impatient too and she was glad when the boy came racing back with the cat food and the milk. 'Give them to the lady,' advised the professor, and put his hand in his pocket again. 'Get yourself and your friends some chips.'

The boy took a delighted look at the money. 'Yer a bit of all right!' he shouted cheerfully as he and his friends scattered down the street...

Which gave Megan the chance to thank her companion all over again for his help, wish him goodnight and watch him drive away before going into her new home to feed the cat and unpack her case.

The cat, nicely full, sat and watched her. He was too thin and uncared for but she thought that with a little pampering he would turn into a splendid animal. 'You haven't a name,' she observed, 'and since you're not a stray but belong here you must have a name. I wonder where you come from and how long you have been wandering around Meredith Street?'

She stroked his grubby head. 'Of course, that's your name: Meredith.'

There was a miserable little yard at the back of the flat where the tenants kept their dustbins and the patch of grass struggled to keep green. She opened the door in the tiny kitchen and went outside but presently crept in again. She locked the door again, opened the small window beside it so that he could get in and out if he wished, put food down for him and wished him goodnight. She wasn't very happy about the window but she wasn't going to turn him out so late in the evening and the brick wall round the yard was very high.

The ward was busy the next day and take-in had started again. She had felt guilty at taking her day off during their busy week but it was Jenny's weekend and she would probably be on duty for very long hours then. She was tired by the evening but she was free until Friday morning. She took the rest of her things to the flat, welcomed by Meredith, and then made up the bed, which pretended to be a divan during the day, cooked herself supper, fed the cat and sat down by the fire to make a list of the things she would need for the supper she had planned for the next day. That done, she turned the divan back into a bed again, had a shower in the cupboard-like apartment squeezed in between the kitchen and the back yard, and, well content, slept soundly with the cat Meredith, who had climbed cautiously on to the end of the bed.

Megan opened an eye as he wriggled into the blankets. 'You need a good wash and brush-up,' she muttered, and then slept again.

CHAPTER TWO

MEGAN got up early, for there was a lot to do. She breakfasted, fed Meredith, tidied her small home and went shopping. A bus took her to the Mile End Road, where she filled her basket and hurried back to the flat. The daffodils she had brought back with her had brightened up the rather dark room and there was a shaft of pale sunlight shining through its window. New curtains, she decided happily as she unpacked the basket, pale yellow and tawny, and some new lampshades instead of the rather severe ones Theatre Sister had favoured. They could wait for a few days; supper was what mattered. She made herself some coffee, buttered a roll, fed the cat again and found an old woolly scarf for him to sit on, then spread her shopping on the table in the tiny kitchen.

She chopped onions for the onion soup, peeled potatoes, cut up courgettes and carrots, trimmed lamb chops, got everything ready to make a baked custard and arranged the Brie and Stilton on a dish. Oscar would be off duty at six o'clock, which meant he would arrive half an hour later than that. She had plenty of time; she made a batch of cheese scones and put them in the oven, then went into the living-room to lay the table and light the fire, then, well satisfied with her efforts, she put on one of her pretty dresses and did her hair and face, made a cup of tea and ate one of the scones and then started to cook. The stove was adequate but there was very little room; it meant cooking the soup first so that there would be room for the other saucepans later. The chops she dressed with a few sprigs of rosemary and put into a warm oven while she made the custard and presently put that in the oven too. She hadn't been sure which wine to buy so she had settled for a rosé and cans of beer; she should have bought a bottle of sherry, she thought worriedly, something she had quite forgotten, but going to look at the table once more she felt satisfied that the tiny room looked welcoming with its one shabby arm-chair by the fireplace with the table beside it. The rest of the room was more or less filled by the dining table under the window, the two chairs with it and the built-in cupboard and shelves along one wall. There was a padded stool and another small table by the divan and with the two lamps switched on the place looked almost cosy. She opened the kitchen window and let Meredith out, promising him his supper when he returned, then she went back to the stove. Oscar would be coming in half an hour or so and it was time to get the vegetables cooked.

Everything was just about ready by half-past six but there was no sign of Oscar; ten minutes went by and she was worrying about everything being overdone when the phone—a necessity laid on by the hospital only for theatre sisters—rang. Oscar sounded very cheerful. 'Megan? Something's come up—you won't mind, will you, if I don't come round? One of the housemen has just got engaged and we're having a bit of a party.'

That was true enough; she could hear laughter and singing in the background and she could hear women's voices too. She reminded herself that there were several women doctors at Regent's before she asked in what she hoped was a matter-of-fact voice if he was coming later.

'Not a chance. We'll be going strong for several hours yet.' He chuckled in what she considered was an infuriating manner. 'I'm glad I'm not on call.'

She boiled silently. 'A pity—supper's all ready...'

'Put the baked beans back in the tin for next time,' said Oscar.

That was a bit too much. She hung up.

The smells from the stove were mouthwatering. She turned off the gas and found that she was shaking with rage and disappointment. She would open the wine and drink the lot, she thought wildly, and was scarcely aware that there were tears running down her cheeks. She wiped them away furiously when there was a knock on the door; Oscar had come after all... she flung the door open and found Professor van Belfeld with the cat Meredith tucked under one arm, standing there.

He didn't wait to be asked in but went past her and put the cat down on the divan. 'He was at the end of the road, a cyclist came round the corner and knocked him down. I happened to be passing. I don't think he's injured, but if you like I'll take a look.'

He glanced at her with casual swiftness so that she hoped he hadn't seen the tears. 'Oh, please—and thank you for rescuing him. I thought it quite safe in the yard. I'll get a little towel...'

The professor took his time; Megan had the chance to wipe her tear-stained cheeks and blow her nose as soundlessly as possible. The only looking-glass was in the tiny shower-room and she had to trust to luck that she looked normal again. She made a mental note to acquire another for the kitchen as soon as possible. She didn't look normal, she looked woebegone and red about her pretty nose, but the professor refrained from comment, merely remarked that the cat had no bones broken although he was probably badly bruised. He lifted him on to the scarf before the fire and stood up.

'You're expecting a guest. I'm sorry if I've held things up in the kitchen.'

'It—it doesn't matter—he's not coming. Oscar—there's a party at the hospital.' Her lip quivered like a small girl's. 'I cooked supper and now there's only me to eat it all.' She gave a sniff and added, 'So sorry...'

The professor took off his coat. 'Would I do instead? Something smells delicious and I'm very hungry,' and when she looked doubtful, 'I had no lunch.'

'Really? You'd like to stay? But haven't you a home...?'

'Yes, yes, of course I have, but there's no one there this evening.'

He sounded very convincing and he didn't spoil it by adding anything to that.

'Well, it would be nice if you stayed. Will your car be all right outside?'

'I left some boys on guard.'

'Won't they get cold?'

'They're sitting inside.' He went to the table and picked up the wine. 'If you have a corkscrew I'll open this.'

She went back to the stove and turned the gas on again and presently served the soup. 'I'm sorry I haven't anything to offer you—no sherry or whisky—I'm not quite settled in yet.'

'This soup needs nothing. You made it yourself?'

'Yes, I like cooking.' It helped a lot to see the soup, so carefully made with its round of toast and parmesan cheese on top, being eaten with such enjoyment. The lamb chops were eaten too, washed down with the rosé, which the professor drank with every appearance of enjoyment. It was perhaps the first time in his life that he had drunk wine at three pounds twenty-five pence a bottle; the price had been on the cork and he suspected that she had chosen it because it was a pretty colour.

He laid himself out to be pleasant and she was surprised to discover that he was a good companion, not saying much and never raising his voice, but what he said was interesting and had nothing to do with hospital life. Here was a different man from the one who had stared down at the broken dish and raked her with such a cold blue gaze. She discovered suddenly that she was enjoying herself. The cheese and biscuits followed the chops and since there wasn't much room to sit anywhere else they had their coffee at the table with the plate of cheese scones between them.

Thinking about it afterwards, Megan wasn't sure what they had talked about; certainly she had learned nothing of the professor's private life, as she hadn't dared to ask questions and he had volunteered no information, although he had told her that he had a dog and a cat, but he had only mentioned them casually while he was taking another look at Meredith, lying at his ease before the fire, comfortably full of supper.

Much to her surprise, he had helped her wash up before he had thanked her quietly for his supper and a pleasant evening, not once saying a word about Oscar—she had been grateful for that—and then he had gone out to his car, sent the boys home gleefully clutching small change, and driven himself away, lifting a casual hand as he went.

There was no chance of seeing Oscar the next day. The usual spate of cases were warded and the ward was full again, and it was a good thing, Megan decided, for it would take her a day or two to get over her disappointment at Oscar's casual treatment. It was two days later before she did see him on her way back from her midday dinner.

'Sorry about the other evening, Megan,' he said cheerfully. 'I knew you would understand. How about tomorrow? I'm off in the evening unless there's any kind of emergency.'

Megan mentally arranged the off duty. 'No good— I'm on duty and I'll be too tired even to open a can of beans.' She gave him a brilliant smile. 'Can't stop— there's a case going to Theatre. Bye.'

In her office she got out the off-duty book and went in search of Jenny. 'I particularly want an afternoon off tomorrow; would you mind changing?'

Jenny was only too glad to agree and Megan sailed back to her office, feeling that at least she had got some of her own back. It wasn't nice of her, she admitted to herself, and indeed she was a kind-hearted and thoughtful girl by nature, but Oscar had upset her, she had to admit, and had made her uneasy. It wasn't as if they saw a great deal of each other, there was no question of that, and didn't absence make the heart grow fonder? Or did it?

There was no sign of the professor, but that was quite normal; he seldom came on to the wards and when he did he wasted no time in conversation unless it was of a professional nature. It was quite by chance that she overheard Mr Bright telling Will Jenkins that the professor had gone off to Holland. 'Won't be back for a few days,' grumbled Mr Bright, 'but I suppose he wants to see his family from time to time.'

So he was married—the thought gave Megan the strange feeling that she had lost something.

Take-in finished and the ward reverted to its normal busy state, without the sudden upheavals of accident cases, and Megan, relenting, spent an evening with Oscar, having a meal at a quiet restaurant near Victoria Park. She enjoyed herself and Oscar was so nice that she felt mean about changing her off duty the week before and when he suggested that he might go to her home with her on her next free weekend she agreed happily.

'I can get a weekend,' he pointed out. 'Heaven knows I'm due for one.'

'That will be marvellous. Can we go home on Saturday morning and stay until Sunday evening?'

He saw her back to the flat and stayed for ten minutes or so. 'Not much of a place, is it?' he pointed out, and she tried not to mind that. She had the new curtains up and cushions to match, fresh flowers and her books on the bookshelves. Even the cat Meredith looked glossy and well fed. A sensible girl, she understood that to a man the flat appeared to lack the comfort and convenience of home, and she contented herself by telling him that she was very happy with it. 'If I want to go to bed early I can,' she explained. 'At the nurses' home there is always a good deal of noise and people popping in and out and playing their cassettes. You'd be surprised how quiet this street is.'

He laughed and kissed her. 'Take care; you'll be turning into a regular old maid unless you look out!'

'That's easily remedied. We could get married.' She didn't know why she had said that and she regretted it when she saw his frown.

'Time enough to talk about that when I've finished here and applied for another post,' he told her, and because he saw that she was feeling awkward, added another kiss to the one that he had already given her.

Megan, left alone, turned the divan into a bed, put on a kettle for a cup of tea and brushed Meredith's coat.

He was filling out nicely and since his accident had prudently stayed in the back yard. He scoffed the saucer of milk she offered him now and composed himself for sleep before the fire, although the minute she turned out the light and got into bed he would creep stealthily on to the end of it and stay there all night.

It was several days later that she saw the professor again. She was going off duty after an exceptionally busy day and she was tired and cross and a little untidy. He and Mr Bright were standing in the entrance hall, deep in some discussion; Mr Bright looked up and called a cheerful, 'Goodnight, Sister Rodner,' and the professor looked at her too, rather as though he couldn't remember where he had met her before, and gave a brief, abstracted nod. She went on her way, feeling put out; he had, after all, eaten a hearty supper at her invitation. She corrected that—his invitation; she hadn't expected that it would lead to a closer relationship, he wasn't close to anyone as far as she knew, but it merited a civil greeting.

She aired her views to Meredith as she got her supper. 'Very rude,' she told him as she stooped to set a saucer of food before him. 'But perhaps he's feeling homesick if he's just back from Holland.'

She and Oscar were to go to her home at the weekend; she had seen him that morning and he had been eager to go. His enthusiasm had astonished and pleased her, for she knew what a lot of arranging had to be done before he could consider himself free for more than a day at a time. They could leave on Friday evening, he had suggested, and be there by ten o'clock, if that wasn't too late for her parents, and she had agreed happily. Tomorrow she would have to find time to buy a cat basket. Meredith had stopped roaming the streets now that he had a good home but left on his own he might stray and she had got fond of him. A little fresh country air would do him good.

Friday began badly; she was entering the hospital when she saw the professor getting out of his car, near enough for them to have exchanged good-mornings, but she was still annoyed with him and swept through the door as though there was no one to be seen for miles around her. He followed her in an elegant, leisurely fashion, smiling a little. He didn't smile a great deal and the head porter gave him a surprised look and observed to one of his underlings that Professor van Belfeld didn't seem quite himself. 'Something must 'ave shook 'im up,' he added weightedly.

On the ward Megan found that the night had gone badly. A patient had fallen out of bed; no one's fault but there needed to be a special report sent in, the medical houseman sent for to examine the lady and the nurses to reassure. It was a bad start to the day, although the patient, a stout lady who had rolled out of bed when she had turned over, had had no injury. Megan, coping with Authority, who wanted to know all about it, found her temper, usually calm, fraying badly. It frayed even more when Mr Bright, due for a ward-round, arrived half an hour late, so that dinners had to be kept hot while he went from bed to bed, taking his time. You would have thought, reflected Megan, seething with impatience, that the smell of fish, mingled with stewed beef and carrots, would help to remind him that the patients had to eat...

Oscar had said that he would be ready to leave by six o'clock and she was hard put to it to get off duty at her usual time. She didn't go to her dinner, but made do with a sandwich and a cup of tea in her office, working through the afternoon so that when Jenny came on duty she was able to leave with an easy mind, hurry to the flat, change, stuff an indignant Meredith into his basket and collect her overnight bag before Oscar came to collect her.

Her mood improved when she saw him; he looked reassuringly ordinary, and obviously he was delighted at the idea of a weekend away from the hospital too. He stowed the cat on the back seat, put her bag in the boot and got in beside her, kissed her briefly and drove off.

'We should get there well before ten o'clock,' he told her. 'Once we can get out of London we'll use the motorway this time.' He turned to smile at her. 'It's a lovely evening too.'

She agreed, feeling better already. 'Is there anything special you want to do? There are some marvellous walks if you feel like it...'

'Let's see how we feel,' he said easily. 'Your family might have some ideas.' He added, 'You look tired; have you had a bad day?'

That was the nice thing about him, she thought—he always remembered that she worked as well as he and took an interest in her days. 'Well, not bad exactly, just lots of small things going wrong. We'd got straightened out by the time I went off duty and Jenny's very capable.'

They talked shop for some time—it relieved the tedium of their slow progress during the rush-hour—but presently when they were clear of the suburbs they fell silent. There's no need to talk, thought Megan; we know each other well enough for there to be no need to make conversation. She felt comfortable with him. The thought flashed through her mind that they were perhaps too comfortable; surely she should feel rather more than that when they were together? It left her uneasy and presently she voiced her doubts.

'Oscar, do you feel excited when I'm with you?' That didn't sound quite right and she tried again. 'Don't laugh—I really want to know.'

They were on the motorway and it was comparatively free of traffic so that he was able to answer her without distraction.

'Megan, dear, of course I won't laugh, and I do understand what you mean. My feeling for you is—how shall I put it?—deep and sincere, but I believe I am not a man to get excited, as you put it. I am happy and content and I believe that we shall settle down very well together.' He glanced at her smiling. 'Does that answer your question?'

She wanted to tell him that it didn't but instead she told him that it did. Perhaps there was no such thing as the kind of romance one read about in books. She twiddled the ring on her finger and told herself that she was happy.

Her mother and father and Melanie were waiting for them when they arrived. They had made good time and since it wasn't yet ten o'clock they had waited supper for them and they sat round the table talking, comfortably aware that the next day was Saturday and there was no hurry to go to work in the morning. Megan, sitting beside Oscar, was pleased to see that he got on so well with Melanie. She smiled at her sister across the table; she had mothered her and shielded her as a child and she loved her dearly. It was a delight to see her talking and laughing so easily with him.

She woke early because it was a habit born of hospital routine, and decided that it was far too soon to get up. She got out of bed and pulled back the curtains. The sun wasn't quite up but the sky was clear and the country around was green and fresh. She drew a contented breath and then let it out with a small gasp. Oscar and Melanie had just left the house by the kitchen door below her window. They were talking softly as they went down the garden to the gate at the end which would lead them to a lane which would take them into the woods beyond the house.

Megan got back into bed and thought about it. Perhaps Oscar hadn't slept well, and, intent on an early morning walk, had met Melanie, who had possibly got up early to get morning tea for everyone. He had talked during supper about bird watching; he might have been going to do just that and Melanie had offered to show him the best places to watch from. She turned over and went to sleep again.

She woke a couple of hours later to find Melanie sitting on the edge of the bed with a cup of tea in her hand, and she sat up, her dark hair hanging in a tangle about her shoulders. 'Where were you and Oscar going?' she asked.

'Did you see us? Why didn't you call—we'd have waited for you. Oscar wanted to see some birds, remember? And he came downstairs while I was in the kitchen—I'd got up early to get the tea so we had a cup and I took him along to Nib's Wood.' She looked anxious. 'You don't mind, Meg?'

'Darling, of course not. As a matter of fact that's what I thought you were going to do. Oscar's nice to be with, isn't he?'

'Oh, yes, he doesn't mind that I'm not witty and amusing...'

'Who does mind?'

'Oh, George at the Manor and the Betts boys at Home Farm and the new clerk in father's office.'

Megan said indignantly, 'They don't say so?'

'Well, not quite, but that's what they mean.'

Megan put her arms round her sister, 'Darling, don't take any notice of them. You're nice as you are and all the nice men—the kind you'll marry—like girls like you.'

'Oh, I do hope so.'

Melanie put a gentle hand on Meredith's head. He had curled up on the end of the bed and not stirred but now he opened his eyes and yawned. 'I'd better get up,' said Megan, 'and see to this monster. Is breakfast ready?'

'Half an hour. What are you going to do today?'

'Show Oscar the village, give Mother a hand, potter in the garden. Oscar works very hard. I dare say he'll like to be left to do his own thing.'

When she got downstairs her mother was in the kitchen dishing up eggs and bacon, and Melanie was making toast.

Megan carried the coffee through to the dining-room and found her father and Oscar there. She stooped to kiss the top of her father's head as he sat in his chair and offered a cheek to Oscar.

He flung an arm round her shoulders. 'I was up early; I've been bird watching,' he told her. 'Melanie was up too and she kindly showed me the best places to go to. I must say the country around here is delightful. I'm almost tempted to turn into a GP and settle down in rural parts,' but when he saw the look on Megan's face he laughed and added, 'But I won't do that, I've set my heart on a good London practice and a senior post in one of the teaching hospitals. Megan knows that, don't you, darling?'

'Yes, of course I do. You'll be so successful that we'll be able to afford a cottage in the country for weekends.' She smiled at him, knowing that he'd set his heart on making a success of his career and understanding that he intended to do just that with a single-minded purpose which could ignore her own wish to live away from London. He deserved success, she thought; he had worked very hard and he was a good doctor. She watched him being gentle with Melanie and felt a glow of gratitude; her sister, usually so painfully shy, was perfectly at ease with him.

Driving back to Regent's on Sunday evening, she asked Oscar, 'You enjoyed yourself? You weren't bored?'

'Good lord, no, it was marvellous. I like your family, Megan. That young brother of yours is a splendid chap.'

'Yes, he is, and he likes you. So does Melanie. You must have seen how shy she is with people she doesn't know well but you got on with her splendidly.'

He didn't answer, she supposed because of the sudden congestion of traffic.

At the hospital he said, 'How about another weekend when I can get one?'

'Lovely. I'll be going again in two weeks but I don't suppose you can manage one as soon as that.'

'Afraid not, but I could try for the weekend after.'

'Let me know in good time. I'll have to alter the off duty but I know Jenny won't mind. Ought you not to go home and see your parents?'

'I'll scrounge a half-day during the week.'

He didn't ask her if she wanted to go with him. Perhaps he had noticed that she and his mother hadn't taken to each other. That would take some time, she reflected as they said goodnight.

Monday morning was busy for there were admissions for operation on the following day, which meant all the usual tests, a visit from the anaesthetist, examinations by painstaking housemen and finally a brief visit from Mr Bright during the afternoon to bolster up his patients' failing spirits and cast an eye over his houseman's reports. The last patient of the four was a thin, tired-looking woman and he spent longer than usual talking to her, putting her at her ease before turning to the papers in his hand.

He paused at the path. lab. report and read it again. 'You've seen this, Sister?' he asked.

'Yes, sir.'

'Most unusual. Be good enough to go to the path. lab. will you, and check with Professor van Belfeld? We shall need to get a supply...'

Megan nipped smartly through the hospital and opened the path. lab. department door. The professor wasn't going to like having one of his decisions questioned.

He was at his desk. She wondered if he sat there all day, for he looked remarkably alert and not in the least tired. He looked up as she knocked and went in. His, 'Yes, Sister?' was politely questioning.

'Mr Bright asked me to check with you—this blood-group report. He thought it was unusual.'

'It is unusual; it is also correct. I checked it personally. You may tell Mr Bright that with my compliments.' He picked up his pen. 'Run along now, I'm rather busy.'

She turned on her heel and made for the door, choking back all the rude words on her tongue. Run along, indeed; who did he think he was?

'Be good enough to close the door firmly as you go out, and tell Mr Bright that I have arranged for a suitable blood donor.'

Megan, a mild girl, was boiling over. Such rudeness... She opened the door and said unforgivably over one shapely shoulder, 'Tell him yourself, sir,' and flounced out haughtily, leaving the door slightly ajar.

Hurrying back to the ward, the enormity of what she had said hit her. She would get the sack; insubordination, she supposed it would be called. Oscar would be angry with her for losing her temper and behaving like a silly child; her parents would be unhappy; she would be given one of those references which damned with faint praise and would end up looking after a geriatric ward in some old-fashioned hospital in the Midlands. Her wild thoughts showed plainly on her face when she got back to the ward and Mr Bright asked, 'Did Professor van Belfeld eat you alive?' He laughed as he said it and she said quickly,

'No, no, Mr Bright. He asked me to tell you that he agreed that it was a most unusual blood-group and that he had arranged for a blood donor.'

'Good man. I don't know what this hospital would do without him.'

Megan mumbled something; maybe the hospital couldn't do without him but she for one could. She tidied the papers Mr Bright had scattered all over the bed and locker and went rigid when the professor's quiet voice speaking its perfect faintly accented English came from behind her.

'I'm sure that Sister Rodner gave you my message, suitably altered to agree with her standard of politeness,' and when Mr Bright laughed he added, 'I hope she will forgive me for my abruptness.'

Megan's charming bosom heaved with pent-up feelings. She was still casting around for a suitable answer to this when he went on, 'I thought it best if I came down to see you—there are a couple of elements in this case which need clarifying.'

Megan had moved away to arrange the bedclothes over her patient. It had been quite unnecessary for him to apologise to her like that and now he had put her in the wrong. She would have to apologise; not that she intended to do that until she knew if he was going to make a complaint about her conduct. The tiresome man. She worried about it for the rest of the afternoon, which was quite unnecessary; it was a pity she hadn't seen the professor sitting back in his chair with a delighted grin on his face as she had flounced through his office door.

By the time she went off duty she had steeled herself to apologise to him but not until the following day. If he was going to make something of it she would be called to Matron's office at nine o'clock. On her way through the hospital she began to compose a speech; it would have to be dignified and apologetic at the same time and she was finding it rather difficult. She was so engrossed that she failed to see the professor coming towards her until they were within a few feet of each other. His first words took her breath.

'Ah, Sister Rodner, I have been expecting your apology.' He sounded pleasantly enquiring and she thought crossly that it would be much easier seriously to dislike him if only he would raise his voice and shout a bit.

'I haven't had much time,' she told him snappily. 'I have every intention of doing so but not until tomorrow.' He was standing before her, blocking a good deal of the passage. 'I'm waiting to see if I have to go to Matron's office.'

'Why?'

'Well, if you have complained about me she won't waste much time before having me in for an interview.' She eyed him wrathfully. 'I shall probably be given the sack or lose my sister's cap or something.'

'My dear young lady, I have no intention of complaining about you. Indeed in your shoes I would have said and done exactly what you did. So you may forget the melodrama and come to work with an easy conscience in the morning.'

He smiled suddenly and just for a moment he didn't look like the austere man she imagined he was. 'It would give me pleasure to take you out to dinner as a token of good faith, but I hesitate to trespass on young Fielding's preserves.'

She was surprised at the flash of regret which she felt. 'It is kind of you to—to think that,' she said carefully. 'I'm sorry I was rude and thank you for being so nice about it.'

'Nice, nice—an English word which means everything or nothing. I am not nice, as you very well know.' He stood aside. 'Goodnight, Sister Rodner.'

She went on her way faintly disturbed and not quite sure why.

Oscar was coming for supper that evening and she made haste home so that she could be ready for him. 'Nine o'clock,' he had said, which gave her time enough. She showered and changed into a grey jersey dress with a bright scarf at the throat, fed the cat, put on a pinny and got to work. A cheese soufflé, a winter salad, crusty french bread and a variety of cheeses. She had some sherry in the house now but she hadn't bought any wine, although there was beer in the cupboard. The room looked cosy enough with the new lampshades casting a kindly pink glow over the cheap furniture and the table with its checked cloth and painted china. Oscar looked a little surprised as he came in. 'I say, this place looks more like it although the furniture's pretty grim. I'm famished...'

The soufflé was a dream of lightness and he ate most of it before starting on the bread and cheese and the bowl of apples. She made coffee and he sat back presently and began to tell her about his day. It wasn't until he got up to go that he observed, 'That was a good meal—I had no idea you could cook, Megan. Did Melanie teach you? I often think of those scones...'

She said evenly, 'Yes, she makes marvellous scones. She's a very good cook.'

He kissed her then, but not how she wanted to be kissed. She wanted to be held close and told that she was a splendid cook too and that he loved her more than anything in the world. Something was not right, she thought, but she didn't know what it was and she made the mistake of asking him.

'Something wrong? Whatever makes you say that? Of course there isn't. I dare say you're tired. Never mind— I've fixed up a weekend; did you change yours?'

'As far as I know.' She watched him walk away and closed the door, then washed her supper things and tidied the room before turning the divan into a bed, feeding Meredith and going to bed, to lie awake listening to his hoarse purr and worrying about her wretched day. Nothing had gone right and she would have enjoyed a good cry, only, as she told herself, she had nothing to cry about.

Take-in started again on Wednesday and since she had changed her weekend with Jenny, she was without that trusty right arm over this weekend, but, as she reminded herself at the end of each busy day, she and Oscar would be going home at the end of the following week. She saw little of him but, as she told the cat Meredith as she got ready to go to work on the last day of take-in, tomorrow they would be back to normal.

Only they weren't. During the afternoon she was told by a sympathetic office sister that there was an outbreak of flu at St Patrick's, who alternated with Regent's, and her ward would have to take in for another week.

There was nothing to be done about it. When she got off duty she went to the porter's lodge and asked if Oscar could see her for a moment and when he came into the entrance hall she told him the bad news at once.

'What bad luck.' He frowned. 'I can't do anything about my weekend; it would mean re-arranging the rota.' His brow cleared. 'I could go to your home on my own, if they'd have me?'

She stifled a feeling of disappointment, feeling mean that she should grudge him the weekend she should have shared with him. 'Of course they will. They'll love to have you. I'll phone Mother.'

'Splendid. I must go, darling. A pity about our weekend.' He sounded cheerful. She watched him go, feeling unreasonably cross.

CHAPTER THREE

MEGAN phoned her mother after supper that evening, sounding more cheerful than she felt.

'How disappointing, darling,' said Mrs Rodner. 'We've been so looking forward to seeing you, and Oscar, of course. But does he really want to come? Surely you'll get some time off during the weekend however busy your ward is; you could have dinner together or just have a quiet time at your flat.'

'Well, yes, Mother, but he's been looking forward to this weekend so much and there's no reason why he should stay here just because I have to.' She added firmly but untruthfully, 'I wouldn't want him to—and he loves being with you all.'

'We shall enjoy having him, dear. Will you be able to manage a day off soon and come home? No need to tell us, just come if you can.'

'After take-in I'll be due to have two days. I'll see what I can do—perhaps next weekend, Mother.'

She rang off, mentally rearranging the off duty; if Jenny had her days off towards the end of take-in, then there was no reason why she herself shouldn't have the weekend. She explained this carefully to Meredith as she got their suppers and was rewarded by a rumbling in his throat which she took to mean that he was pleased.

At her home her mother put down the receiver and turned to Mr Rodner, sitting behind his newspaper. 'George,' she said, loudly enough to make him put the paper down, 'Oscar's coming on his own; Meg can't come—extra take-in or something. Wouldn't you have thought that he'd have wanted to stay there with her? She does get off duty even when they're busy and they could have gone out together.' She frowned. 'George, are you listening? Do you think...have you noticed Melanie and Oscar together? I'm not very happy about that. I wish Megan and Oscar could get married while they're still...'

She paused and her husband said quietly, 'In love, my dear? That would be a mistake, wouldn't it? Yes, I've noticed Melanie and Oscar—these things happen and there's nothing we can do to help.' He picked up his paper again. 'Patience, my dear, and let things take their own course.'

Mrs Rodner glared at him. 'Men,' she observed. 'What about our Meg?'

'Meg is twenty-eight...'

'I know that, and she'll be on the shelf before we know where we are and she is so lovely and such a dear girl.'

'One day a man to match her will turn up, my dear. As I have said, patience.'

Megan had little time to regret her weekend; the ward was still full from the previous week's take-in, and now she was putting up beds down the middle and sending those who were well enough to sleep in other wards. Everyone seemed bent on having an accident that weekend, she observed to Jenny. Men's Surgical was just as busy, and, naturally enough, so was Theatre. Hurrying back from her dinner on Sunday, she went full tilt into the professor, walking with measured stride in the opposite direction. He put out an arm to right her, remarking as he did so, 'You should look where you're going, Sister,' a statement which in no way soothed her.

'Sorry, sir, we're rather busy.'

'Your weekend, is it not?'

'I had to change it.' She sidled round his vast person, ready to nip away.

'A pity. Young Fielding was to have had a weekend too, was he not?'

She wondered fleetingly at his interest. 'Yes.'

'Going to spend it at your home?'

'Yes.' Something in his quiet voice made her add, 'Well, he's there, actually, I mean he doesn't get many weekends and my family like him...'

'Ah, yes, indeed. Don't let me keep you, Sister Rodner.'

Which, seeing that she hadn't been able to get past him, seemed unnecessary.

The long day ended at last and she went back to Meredith's company and a sketchy supper. She was getting ready for bed when Oscar phoned.

He was full of his delightful weekend.

'What did you do?' asked Megan.

'Oh, this and that. We walked a bit and drove over to Wing to see some garden or other, I've forgotten to whom it belonged, then we had lunch in a local pub and got back in time for tea. Been busy?'

'So-so. I'm glad you had a good time.' She wanted to ask who had gone with him—the whole family or Melanie alone? Not that she minded, she told herself stoutly, only it would have been nice if he had told her. He wasn't going to. He enthused over her mother's cooking, suggested that they might meet for a drink when they were free and then wished her goodnight. He hadn't mentioned Melanie once. She lay in bed and worried about that. They had seemed to get on so well together— surely they hadn't taken a dislike to each other? Or was

Melanie ill? She found the thought so disquieting that she picked up the receiver and phoned her mother.

Her mother's voice sounded warmly in her ear. 'Darling, I phoned you twice but you weren't there. You've been busy? Has Oscar got back yet?'

'He rang me just now. He had a lovely time and he loved your cooking. Mother, is Melanie ill?'

'Good heavens, no, whatever made you think that she was?'

'Well, Oscar didn't mention her at all—they haven't disagreed or anything, have they? I was so glad that she liked him but you know how she retires into her shell if she thinks someone doesn't like her.'

'Darling, she's fine, and I'm sure she enjoyed the weekend as much as we all did. I dare say that Oscar had so much to say that he just didn't get around to mentioning her.'

'Oh, that's all right, then. Silly of me to fuss. I think I can manage a day after Wednesday and I'll drive home. I've a day or two owing to me then.'

'That will be lovely, Meg. Goodnight, dear.'

'Goodnight, Mother.' She hung up and got back into bed and since it had turned rather chilly the cat Meredith sidled up until he was curled into the circle of her arm. He felt very comforting.

The workload lessened after Sunday and since several patients were to be discharged Megan was able to have the beds down the centre of the ward taken away and she even had one or two empty ones. She sent Jenny on days off on Tuesday as well as some of the student nurses; she had part-time staff nurses, married ladies who were willing to do extra hours while Jenny was away, and she cheerfully cut her own free time, knowing that she would be able to take two days off herself when Jenny was back.

She went off duty on Friday evening, leaving a quiet ward behind her with only routine admissions and nothing which Jenny couldn't handle. Oscar had rung her on the ward and suggested that they might meet for half an hour after duty. 'I can't really leave the hospital, but I'll come over to the Pot and Feather and we can have a drink.'

He wouldn't be free until after six o'clock, so she went to the flat, showered and changed into a tweed skirt and sweater, fed Meredith and went back to the hospital to wait for Oscar. She disliked going into pubs on her own and there was still time before he would be free.

While she was waiting she roamed round the hall. It was rather a dreary place with a high vaulted ceiling, an endless floor of marble and some large oil-paintings of eminent men hung at intervals on its panelled walls. The portraits were of dead and gone medical men, all looking stern and severe, and clever. She was peering at a former governor of the hospital standing by a small table, his hand on a weighty book, frowning out of his frame at the less exalted persons about him.

'He might have been a good husband and then father,' observed Megan, talking to herself because the vast place discomfited her.

'You are doubtful of that, Sister Rodner?'

The professor had come upon her softly and she jumped and turned at the same time. 'Good evening, sir. Yes, I am, I think he had a nasty temper.'

'Is this how you spend your off-duty hours?' he asked.

'Of course not, I'm waiting for Oscar. He's got half an hour to spare.'

'You will go to your home tomorrow?'

'Yes. How did you know?' She gave him a surprised look and found him smiling.

'Mr Bright mentioned it. I am going to Oxford tomorrow. Is half-past eight too early for you? I will come to your flat?'

'Too early? Come to my flat?' echoed Megan, her pretty mouth agape.

'Have I not made myself clear?' The professor sounded testy. 'I will drop you off on my way.'

'That's awfully kind of you, but I was going to drive myself...'

He ignored this. 'I asked you if half-past eight was too early for you.' He wasn't going to take no for an answer, she could see, and besides, the thought of driving in comfort in a Rolls-Royce was tempting. She said cautiously, 'I shall have the cat Meredith with me.'

'So I should imagine,' and then impatiently, 'Well?'

'Thank you, I should like a lift if it's not going out of your way. I'll be ready.'

'Good. Good evening to you, Sister Rodner.'

He had gone as quietly as he had come and a few minutes later Oscar joined her.

She began at once after the briefest of greetings. 'Oscar——'

'You want to know about the weekend?' he interrupted her. 'Let's go over to the pub, we can't talk here.' He marched her over to the Pot and Feather, and sat her down in the crowded bar. 'What'll it be?' he asked.

'A large tonic with lots of ice and lemon.'

'A dash of gin?'

She shook her head, then watched him as he made his way to the bar. He looked different. Usually he was rather quiet after a day's work but now he looked—she wasn't quite sure how he looked. Excited? Happy? Had he missed her so much? She smiled at the thought and when he came back said, 'Well, now tell me all about the weekend.'

He embarked on a detailed account and she should have been satisfied with that, but somehow there was something not quite right. Despite his obvious pleasure in recalling it, he was wary, almost as though he was afraid of saying something he didn't want her to know. Besides, he gave her little chance to ask questions and when they had had their drinks he said he would have to go back to Regent's. 'I said half an hour and I must set a good example to the housemen.'

She got up with him. 'We must have another weekend as soon as you can manage it,' she suggested.

'Not much hope of that, darling, and if I get the odd day off I really must go home.'

'Yes, of course. We'll wait for a while. I'm going home tomorrow.' They had reached the hospital and she began, 'I was going to drive down——'

'Why not?' he asked. 'I must fly.' There was no one around, so he gave her a light kiss on her cheek. 'Give my love to everyone.'

He was gone. I'll tell him when I get back, decided Megan.

She went back to the flat, got supper for herself and Meredith, packed an overnight bag, watched suspiciously by him, and set his basket ready. 'You're going in a Rolls-Royce,' she told him, 'and mind you behave yourself.'

The cat yawned.

It was April now and the mornings were light. She was up early to get breakfast, get into a new outfit she hadn't yet worn—a little grey jacket with a long pleated skirt in shades of grey and blue with a hint of pale green and a white cotton shirt. She had spent more than she had intended on it but she knew that it suited her; besides, as she told Meredith, 'It is spring and if I don't wear it now there's not much point in having it.'

If she didn't wear it now, she added silently, the professor wouldn't see her in it, although why that should matter she didn't know.

He arrived at exactly half-past eight and from the casual glance he gave her as he wished her good morning she might just as well have run up a little something from dishcloths. He wasted no time but stowed Meredith on the back seat, put her bag in the boot, got in beside her and drove off. Almost as though he regretted offering her a lift. The thought made her feel shy and awkward and, since he was concentrating on getting out of the city as quickly as possible and she could think of nothing to say, the first ten minutes or so went by in silence. Finally she ventured, 'It's a nice morning.' Only when she said that she remembered that he had no use for the word nice.

She was surprised when he said in a friendly voice, 'A delightful morning. How long are you to be at home? And may I call you Megan?'

'I've got the weekend off, and please call me Megan if you would like to.'

'Thank you. I am returning to Regent's on Sunday evening. I will call for you very shortly after six o'clock.'

'Well, that's kind of you, but you do have to go out of your way...'

'A few miles. Your family expect you this morning. I think it likely that we shall arrive a bit earlier than you would have done if you had driven yourself.'

'Well, a Rolls does go faster than my little car,' Megan said matter-of-factly. 'It's very comfortable, isn't it? And very large.' She glanced sideways at him and added seriously, 'Of course, you do need a big car, don't you?'

He gave a rumble of laughter. 'Indeed I do.'

It was a chance to find out more about him. 'Do you take it to Holland when you go?'

She wasn't looking at him and didn't see his faint smile. 'Oh, yes, I need it there.'

'For your family?' she asked, greatly daring, afraid of being snubbed.

'For my family.' Not quite a snub, but something in his quiet voice stopped her from asking any more questions. She didn't need to, she reflected, and began to weave her thoughts into his life; married with a wife—who would be a handsome woman to match his height and always beautifully dressed—and there would be children, three or four of them. It was a pity that she didn't know where his home was, because she could have imagined that as well.

'You are silent,' observed the professor, and she went a guilty pink, for all the world as though she had spoken her thoughts out loud.

She made haste to say something, no matter what, and in fact she said in a matter-of-fact-way, 'I can't think of anything interesting or amusing to talk about and I don't think you would like me to—to waffle...'

'I am relieved to find that you understand me so well.' He had turned off the main road and taken a cross-country route without pausing to look at signposts. Megan thought that he must have studied the map closely, for he hadn't asked her the way once. When they came to the narrow downhill lane to the village he turned the big car into it without a pause.

'Have you been here before?' she asked.

'No. Why do you ask?'

'Well, you know the way so well, and it's a bit complicated once you leave the main road.'

'I have a map.' A remark which put an end to the conversation once again.

He went through the village, swept the Rolls gently up to the front door and got out to open her door. Before she could say anything the front door opened and her mother came towards them.

'Darling, how nice and early.'

She looked at the professor and smiled with a questioning look, and Megan said, 'Mother, this is Professor van Belfeld—he very kindly gave me a lift. He's on his way to Oxford.'

Mrs Rodner shook hands. 'How very nice of you. Come in and have some coffee.'

The professor smiled at her. 'Thank you, Mrs Rodner, but I have to be in Oxford very shortly.' He glanced at Megan. 'Until six o'clock on Sunday,' he reminded her, handed her her bag and Meredith and got back into the car.

They watched him go and Mrs Rodner put an arm through her daughter's.

'What a charming man. He's very large, isn't he? And not very talkative.'

'Charming,' echoed Megan. 'Heavens, Mother, the nurses run a mile when they seen him coming...'

'He's never unkind to them?'

'No. No, nothing like that—they're in awe of him, I suppose; he never says much, you see, even when he's angry about something. He can't stand carelessness or things getting forgotten.'

They wandered into the house, Megan carrying the basket with Meredith breathing in a frustrated way through his little window. 'You're not in awe of him?' asked Mrs Rodner.

'Goodness me, no. In fact I've been rather rude to him once or twice! He's always right...'

'How very annoying, darling, but men always are. Let's have coffee. Your father has had to go into Thame, but he'll be back for lunch. I'm glad you can stay until Sunday evening. Do you suppose your professor would like tea or coffee when he calls for you?'

'He might, but I don't think so. We don't mix socially at all.' She was a truthful girl. 'Well, hardly ever.' And was having supper at her little flat mixing socially? She hardly thought so.

'He's a very large man,' remarked her mother again, pouring coffee.

Megan was letting Meredith out of his basket. 'Yes. Where's Melanie?'

'It's her turn to help with the flowers at the church. She'll be back presently.'

They sat facing each other at the kitchen table while Meredith prowled.

'Oscar did enjoy his weekend,' said Megan.

'He fits in very well—such an easy young man to entertain. A pity you weren't able to come too, Meg.' She eyed her beautiful daughter's face. 'You're rather pale, dear—you've been working too hard.'

'Well, yes, but now I've two whole days to be idle. I thought I'd take a fortnight's holiday at the end of June. Are you and Father going away? Melanie said something about going to Brittany; we might go together.'

'Can't Oscar get some time off with you, and shouldn't you pay another duty visit to his people?'

'He told me he hasn't a chance of leave for several months—the odd weekend perhaps.' She cut a hunk of the cake her mother had put on the table and bit into it. 'I don't think Mrs Fielding will invite me unless she has to. She doesn't like me and I don't like her. I dare say it will be all right if we keep away from each other and just meet when we have to.'

Mrs Rodner looked doubtful. 'Darling, I'm not sure...' She broke off as Melanie came in, gave Megan a hug and sat down beside her.

'I say, someone at the church said they saw you in a Rolls-Royce going through the village. Was it you?'

'Yes. The professor of pathology was going to Oxford and gave me a lift.'

'Is he nice? Young? Good-looking?'

'Well, I'm not sure if you'd like him.' Megan reflected that her shy sister would retire even deeper into her shell if they should ever meet. 'He's not young. I've no idea... about forty, I suppose, and he's good-looking and he's rather reserved.'

'He has very bright blue eyes, the faintest accent because he's Dutch and he's one of the largest men I've ever seen,' said her mother.

Both girls laughed. 'Mother, I didn't know you were so observant,' said Megan.

'He sounds interesting. What a pity Oscar couldn't come with you, Meg.'

'No chance of that for a while, Melly. He'll squeeze out a weekend when he can—even a day. It very much depends on what's on the wards.' She smiled at her. 'You had a lovely weekend, didn't you?'

'Heavenly. I took him to those gardens—that place near Wing, the daffodils were gorgeous and we had lunch at the pub there.' Melanie's pretty little face shone with pleasure at the remembrance.

'You get on well with Oscar, don't you, love?' asked Megan.

'Oh, yes. You don't mind, Meg?'

'Mind? Of course not. I would have minded very much if you had disliked each other on sight, and Oscar gets so little time in which to enjoy himself away from his work.'

'Well, now you've got that flat he'll have somewhere to go when he can snatch an hour,' said Mrs Rodner comfortably. Only she didn't feel comfortable; she looked at her two daughters, both unaware of what was happening to them, and there was no way of telling them. They would have to discover it for themselves, and since they were both fond of each other they would both be hurt.

She got up from the table. 'I thought I would make a rhubarb pie—it would be nice,' she said. 'Will one of you pick some for me? There's plenty under the buckets at the bottom of the garden. Meredith might like to go with you.'

The two girls, happily unaware of her thoughts, went off into the kitchen garden with the cat at their heels. They picked the rhubarb then sat down on an old wheel-barrow to crunch the radishes that they had pulled.

'They've had the horses out at Cobb's Farm,' said Melanie. 'There are mushrooms in the bottom field, and Mr Cobb said I could have any I liked to pick.'

'There can't be many at this time of year, but we might go and look before breakfast tomorrow. Church in the morning?'

'Oh, yes. I made Oscar go,' Melanie laughed. 'He said he hadn't been for ages, but he did it to please me.'

Megan ate another radish. 'Good for you, love. We'd better take this rhubarb to Mother or we shan't get a pie for lunch.'

Megan didn't waste a moment of her weekend; the weather remained springlike and warm and she spent hours pottering around the garden, weeding and planting and eating her mother's splendidly cooked meals. She had time to think too, and away from the hospital it seemed so much easier to do that clearly. The vague uncertainties she had been worrying about became unimportant, the subtle change in Oscar's manner towards her became a figment of her imagination, and by Sunday evening she had sorted out her feelings, told herself that she had been overtired and fancied things which hadn't happened at all. 'A load of rubbish,' she assured Meredith cheerfully, and didn't allow her thoughts to dwell on the fact that Oscar hadn't phoned at all over the weekend. Then, of course, there was really no reason why he should, only that he had formed that habit when she went home for weekends on her own.

Mindful of the professor's weakness for punctuality, she was ready, with Meredith in his basket, by six o'clock. They were all in the drawing-room, exchanging last-minute chat, when they heard the car whisper to a halt and Mrs Rodner stood up. 'I'll go,' she said, and left the room before anyone could say anything, to return after a few moments with the professor looming behind her. Looking at him, Megan reflected that if one didn't know him one would suppose him to be a mild man incapable of uttering any but the kindest of words. He shook her father's hand with every show of pleasure, gave her a nod in greeting, and took the hand Melanie held out to him.

He took it gently and gave her a smile of such charm that she smiled back. 'I've heard of you from Megan,' he told her in a voice as gentle as his hand clasp. 'You must have enjoyed having her at home, even for such a short time; the weather has been specially good too.'

It surprised Megan that her shy sister answered him without her usual shyness. 'I wish she were at home all the time—we went mushroom-picking before breakfast.'

'The best time of the day. Let us hope that the weather will be just as kind when Megan comes again.'

He didn't linger and after another five minutes' talk with her mother and father asked Megan if she was ready, picked up Meredith's basket and went out to the car with her. Beyond the nod and his question he hadn't spoken to her, although as he opened the car door for her he gave her a thoughtful look. Megan, who had missed the look, thought waspishly that she need not have bothered to have worn the new outfit again; a sack would have done for all the notice he had taken of her. The guilty thought that it shouldn't matter to her—an engaged girl—what the professor thought, anyway, sent the colour into her cheeks so that her companion, getting into the car beside her, cast a look of thoughtful appreciation at her pretty face before turning the key in the car and waving to the little group standing there in the porch. Megan waved too, wrestling with mixed feelings: regret at leaving home once again, pleasure in the company of the professor and a sudden eagerness to see Oscar.

Melanie went back into the house but Mr and Mrs Rodner lingered in the garden. 'He's in love with her,' said Mrs Rodner in a pleased voice.

Her husband took her arm. 'Really? Has he told you so?' He sounded amused.

'Of course not. He won't tell anyone, certainly not our Meg, until he is good and ready.'

'How do you know this, my dear?'

'He didn't even look at her when we came in, just nodded, but didn't you see the way he stared down at her as she got into the car?'

'Well, no, my dear, I can't say that I did, and if you're right, and I must say I find it most unlikely, what about Oscar?'

'He fell in love with Melanie the moment he set eyes on her and she with him. Meg doesn't know that yet, but she knows there's somehow something that's not quite right. I did tell you...'

'Yes, dear, and I suggested that you had patience.'

'Well, I am having patience, only I don't want Meg hurt. I don't think she's really in love with Oscar, not deeply, but all the same she'll feel slighted.'

'Melanie will be upset too.' Mr Rodner turned to his wife and marched her back into the house. 'Let us have coffee and try and forget this; after all, it is pure conjecture.'

On the porch, Mrs Rodner paused to say, 'You liked him...?'

'Yes, I did.'

'There you are, then,' declared Mrs Rodner, clinching the matter.

The professor had very little to say on the way back to London and that was of a trivial nature. Megan, searching her head for something to talk about, grew more and more silent and was thankful that the professor seemed perfectly at ease without the need for conversation. It was only as he drew up before her flat that he said, 'You have all you want? You will allow me to come in with you and make sure that everything is as it should be?'

'Thank you, but there is no need...'

He had helped her out of the car and collected the cat basket and her bag—now he took the door key from her, opened the door and switched on the light.

The little place looked dark and chilly. He bent to light the gas fire and shut the door behind her, let the cat out of his basket and went to examine the back door and the window in the kitchen.

'Would you like coffee—or tea?' asked Megan, quite expecting him to refuse.

'Tea would be delightful.' He put the kettle on as he spoke and she took off her jacket and dug into her bag for the cake her mother had baked, put cups and saucers on a tray and warmed the teapot.

The place looked better already; the lampshades cast a kindly glow over its shabbiness and the gas fire, old-fashioned though it was, gave out a pleasant heat. 'Do sit down,' she begged him, and fetched a plate and a knife. 'Mother always gives me a cake to bring back. Will you have some?'

The tray between them and Meredith sitting at her feet, they drank the pot dry and ate a good deal of the cake.

Presently the professor got up to go. They had been talking about nothing much but now he said, 'Your sister is a very pretty girl but extremely shy, is she not?'

'Yes, you noticed that, didn't you? But not shy with everyone—she liked you.'

'Unlike the nurses at Regent's, she is not afraid of me.' He smiled as he spoke.

'Oh, that's a silly kind of legend about you. You're up on that top floor, you see, and you're so very large. When you go onto the wards they get a bit nervous...'

'Because I'm large?'

'Partly, I suppose, and partly because you're quiet even when you're annoyed about something.'

'I must mend my ways.' He had his hand on the door. 'Don't thank me for the lift—it is I who thanks you. Your company was a pleasure.'

He bent suddenly and kissed her on her surprised mouth. 'Goodnight, Megan.'

She stood still, watching the door close behind him and then listening to the sound of the car driving almost silently away.

'Well!' said Megan, and again, 'Well!' She bent to pick up Meredith and sat down with him on her lap. She had enjoyed the kiss, there was no denying that, and since she had done nothing to encourage such behaviour she told herself that it wasn't necessary to feel guilty about it. She did feel guilty, though, and got up and picked up the receiver and rang Oscar's number at the hospital.

He answered at once. 'You're back—did you have a good weekend? Was everyone all right?'

'They're all fine. Have you been busy? Any chance of a few hours off this week? Even a half-day?'

'I've fixed a day off on Wednesday; I'm going home. I'll try and get an hour or two off one evening. The medical side's chock-a-block and I'm on call.'

'I won't keep you, Oscar. Let me know if you're free and I'll try and fix my off duty. Goodnight, dear.'

She hung up, her mind already busy with possibilities if they could manage an evening together. Perhaps dinner out somewhere? Or should she try once more to cook supper for them both at the flat? She got ready for bed, put everything ready for the morning and lay in the dark, vaguely bothered about something, only she didn't know what that something was.

'It can't be anything much,' she told Meredith, curled up beside her, 'or I'd know, wouldn't I?'

A satisfactory answer: she went to sleep at once.

The ward was relatively quiet when she got to it in the morning. Three cases for operation but an equal number of discharges, which was a good thing since it would be take-in again on Wednesday. She took the report, went through the case sheets with Jenny, did her morning round and went to the office to deal with the paperwork. She had given herself an afternoon off duty so that Jenny could have an evening before her days off and since the operation cases had all gone to Theatre and were back again by one o'clock she felt free to go back to the flat after her dinner in the canteen.

To her friends' enquiries as to whether she had enjoyed her weekend she replied cheerfully that she had had a splendid time, but she didn't tell them that she had had a lift from the professor; even friends gossiped and she could imagine how the hospital grapevine would embellish the news so that soon it would have the pair of them going down the aisle and Oscar a broken man.

She gave the flat a good clean when she got there and then went shopping. The general stores at the end of the street sold just about everything; she stocked up and went back to make herself tea, feed Meredith and put everything ready for her supper when she got back home that evening.

The ward was still quiet and she had enough nurses on duty. She wrote the report, checked the operation cases, talked to anxious relations and did the medicine round, and then gave the report to the night nurses before going off duty. It had been quite a nice day, she reflected on her way home. She wondered if the professor had had a nice day too; only of course nice was a word she knew he didn't approve of.

Take-in began quietly, which was a good thing because Jenny wouldn't be back until the next day. Megan went off duty that evening satisfied that the day had gone as well as could be expected, cooked her supper, attended to Meredith and washed her smalls and then sat down with a book. She had barely opened it before the phone rang.

'It's me,' said Melanie ungrammatically, 'Meg, guess who came today? You never will, anyway: Oscar. He said he had meant to go home but at the last minute he decided that he wanted a day in the country so he came here. We had such a lovely day.'

Megan found her voice. 'Melly, how very nice for you. Did you go walking?'

'Yes. Miles and miles. He's only been gone about an hour. Did he tell you he was coming?'

'No, love, but I've been on duty since eight o'clock this morning, so he wouldn't have had the chance. I know he wasn't too keen to go home. I expect he'll give me a ring when he gets in.'

'He did say he'd fetch me one day so that I can see your flat, Meg. May I visit you? One day when you're free I'd love to see it.'

'Of course you can come. I'll let you have a few days to choose from. Do you want to stay the night? I could get a room for you...'

'Oscar said he'd drive me back.' When Megan didn't answer, she said, 'Meg, you're still there? I expect you're tired. Goodnight, dear.'

Megan put down the receiver. 'How silly of me not to have seen it,' she told Meredith. 'They're just right for each other, aren't they?' A tear trickled down her cheek and she wiped it away angrily. 'Perhaps he loved me a little, but I don't suppose he was ever in love as well. I've been pretty silly too.' Another tear crept down. She didn't wipe it away this time but picked up Meredith and cried all over him.

CHAPTER FOUR

UNLIKE the heroines in romantic fiction, Megan didn't stay awake all night; she mopped her face, mopped a damp Meredith, got into bed and went to sleep for the simple reason that she had had a long day and she was tired. To say that she awoke refreshed would be quite another matter, and while she dressed and drank her tea she struggled to achieve a state of mind in which she could think sensibly what was best to do. 'I'd better see Oscar as quickly as possible,' she told Meredith as she portioned out his breakfast and bit into a slice of toast, 'although I'd much rather not! I must be very calm and sensible too.'

She went to peer at her face in the looking-glass; she looked a hag, she told her reflection. If anyone asked what was the matter she would have to say that she had a cold. A careful make-up might have helped but she had no time.

The ward had been busy overnight, which was a good thing, for the report was rather longer than usual and there was a case in Theatre and a street accident coming up from Casualty. There was, thank heaven, no time for anyone to look at her. She attacked the day's work with her usual energy, satisfied that she looked just the same as usual. Not quite, perhaps, because at dinner her friends stared at her rather hard and asked her what was the matter.

'You look as though someone had knocked you on the head, Meg,' said someone.

'Nothing as dramatic. I've got a cold starting, I think.'

A remark they all accepted without demur. She went back to her ward relieved to think that even if her heart was broken, and she supposed that it was, no one need know. It was a pity that this comforting thought was shattered by the professor, coming the other way and stopping in front of her.

'What is the matter with you?' he demanded in his quiet voice.

'Nothing, sir,' she snapped. 'Just a cold...'

'Don't talk nonsense.'

It was too much, her lip quivered and she sniffed back tears and glared at him. 'It's not nonsense.'

He stood looking down at her, considering. 'You are off duty this evening? We will have dinner together and you shall tell me about it.'

'I must see Oscar.' She remembered her manners. 'But thank you for asking me.'

'There is no point in seeing Oscar in your present frame of mind. We will dine together and you will tell me about this obvious disaster which has turned you into a whey-faced, heavy-eyed young woman not fit to run her ward.'

'Of course I can run my ward,' she told him furiously, 'and you have no business interfering with my—my life.'

'No, no, you are mistaken; I merely offer my services as a father confessor, a shoulder to weep on, or, if you prefer, the disinterest of a stranger.'

She was thinking how to answer this when he said, briskly, 'Well, I can't stand around gossiping. I will call for you at half-past seven this evening.'

He was yards away before she found her tongue.

She was an excellent ward sister but that afternoon she excelled herself. Not fit to run a ward, indeed, she reflected crossly, casting an eye over her well-cared-for patients. He had no idea what he was talking about.

She went off duty half an hour late, sorely tempted to phone Oscar; indeed, if she had seen him on her way through the hospital she might very well have demanded that they should have a talk there and then, but there was no sign of him and she went to the flat to make herself a pot of tea, feed Meredith and search her wardrobe for something to wear. She did it all mechanically, her mind on Oscar, willing him to ring her up while she changed into a dark green taffeta skirt and white crêpe blouse with long full sleeves, the kind of outfit which would look right wherever the professor was taking her. She covered it with a three-quarter-length wool coat with a swing back in the same green as the skirt, found black court shoes and a small hand bag and on an impulse lifted the receiver to phone Oscar's number at Regent's.

She was dialling the number when the door was thumped and she put it down again, feeling guilty. The professor came in, without speaking, adjusted the receiver, which she had failed to put back properly, and remarked gently, 'Just in time, am I?' His eyes searched her face. 'Well, go ahead and phone him if you wish to. There's plenty of time.' He sighed. 'I can always cancel our table.'

'No. No, don't do that.' She was aware suddenly that she was hungry as well as unhappy. 'I'm quite ready.'

He had picked up Meredith. 'This little chap's turned into a fine fellow. He does you credit, Megan.' He put the cat down and opened the door and she went past him, aware of window curtains twitching all around her. Nothing much happened in the drab little street; a Rolls-Royce was an event to be discussed on the doorsteps in the morning. She got into the car and he shut her door and got in beside her.

'Are your neighbours friendly?' he asked.

'Well, I don't see much of them except good morning and good evening; they—they are interested if I go out...'

'Naturally.' He drove away. 'You could have waved.'

She laughed. 'They wouldn't have liked that; they think I can't see them peeping.'

They didn't actually talk much; just a little about the weather, odds and ends of hospital news, the chance of a fine summer. By the time he stopped in Charlotte Street she had lost the shyness she had felt when he had arrived. The restaurant was French and famous and they were shown to a table nicely secluded but in an excellent position in the glamorous room. Megan, looking around her, was glad that she was dressed to suit her opulent surroundings. As for the professor, he had hardly glanced around him but sat, very much at his ease, elegant in his dark grey suit and silk tie. He was no stranger to the place, thought Megan as the *maître d'* bent to murmur in his ear.

Over their drinks she studied the menu. Even an unhappy girl had to eat and she was hungry. She chose lobster mousse, lamb cutlets with basil and Madeira sauce with Auvergne potato purée; the professor chose the lobster and a tournedos cooked in red wine with shallots, and ordered wine without fuss or reference to the wine-list before beginning a conversation which needed very little reply on her part. She ate her dinner with a good appetite, drank two glasses of the wine she was offered, and only when coffee was set before them did he say, 'Now, what is all this about?'

'Aren't you afraid that I might burst into tears?' It was amazing what two glasses of wine could do to boost one's ego.

'No, if I had thought that I would not have brought you here.' He spoke casually, which made it seem easier to start.

'It's Oscar. He's fallen in love with Melanie and I'm sure she's in love with him only I don't think she's realised it. He—he told me that he was going home to see his people yesterday, but instead he spent the day at my home and he didn't tell me. I haven't seen him since he got back, and I haven't phoned him either. I—I don't know how I feel. Melanie is a darling, and I'd like her to be happy.' She poured them each more coffee. 'I thought Oscar loved me; he's not a demonstrative man but all the same...I expected we would be happy together. I'm sure he's fond of me but that's not quite the same as being passionately in love, is it?'

'And you, Megan, are you passionately in love with him?'

She went pink. 'I suppose I thought that our affection for each other was enough, I don't suppose there's such a thing as passionate love in real life. Perhaps now and again, like Oscar and Melanie, I mean when you can't help yourself even if it upsets everything.'

She fell silent and when he didn't speak she said, 'I feel rather as though I've come up against a blank wall. I've no idea what to do.'

'It surprises me that a young woman of normal intelligence can allow her common sense to be swamped in sentiment——'

'Well, really——' began Megan.

'A singularly pointless interruption,' observed the professor. 'I seldom give advice but if I might suggest—

go home and talk to your sister, make sure that she really loves Oscar before you break with him. Unlikely though it seems, it may be a flash in the pan.'

'But I haven't got days off due until the weekend after next.'

'So much the better. You will have the time to simmer down and be able to discuss the matter in a logical manner.'

'What about Oscar? I see him quite often.'

'I feel sure that you can find excuses for not seeing him, although it would make good sense to see something of him and—er—form your own opinion of the situation.'

'Where did you learn to speak such good English?' asked Megan, who had been wondering that but hadn't meant to voice the thought. She blushed and he smiled a little.

'We had an English nanny—we still have her—and I spent several years at Cambridge.'

'Oh, well, that's why. I didn't mean to be inquisitive; it just popped out.' She added, 'Thank you for being so kind. I didn't mean to tell anyone... I'll do as you say, and thank you for your advice.' She hesitated. 'I'm not really whey-faced, am I?'

He answered her seriously, although there was a gleam in his eyes.

'It seemed to me that drastic means were needed to prevent you bursting into tears in a corridor frequented by almost everyone in the hospital.'

'Oh, I see. That was very thoughtful of you.'

He smiled. 'I have long ago learned how to discourage threatened tears.'

Did his wife cry a great deal, she wondered, or was he thinking of small daughters? She very much wanted to know but probably he had learned how to deflect un-welcome questions too.

They went back presently and when he stopped at her flat she didn't ask him in. He got out with her and opened her door and switched on the light just as he had done before, giving the kitchen a quick look and the window and then listening a little impatiently to her thanks before going to the door, wishing her goodnight and driving himself away before she had shut the door. 'He didn't want to be asked in anyway,' she assured Meredith.

She didn't see him after that for several days and she wasn't sure if she was pleased about that or not. She met Oscar on her way to X-Ray and behaved as she always did towards him although it cost an effort and he was quite obviously labouring under a feeling of guilt. It would have been nice if she could have told the pro-fessor how well she had acquitted herself, but there was no sign of him, only on the evening before she was going home as she and Oscar walked across to the pub he passed them in his car, going into the hospital forecourt. He lifted a hand as he went by and Megan, catching a fleeting glimpse of his face, imagined that he was smiling.

The professor had been quite right, of course; by the time she got home she had calmed down sufficiently to be able to tackle the problem of herself and Oscar without wishing to burst into tears at the least mention of it. She took her bag and Meredith out of her car and went indoors, to be met by her mother coming from the kitchen.

'Hello, love. How nice to see you again.' Mrs Rodner spoke cheerfully and looked uneasy. 'Melanie had to go over to Cobb's Farm, but she'll be back presently.'

Megan gave her mother a hug. 'It's all right, Mother. I do know about her and Oscar and you don't need to worry, only I want to talk to her first before I say anything to him.'

'Darling, your father and I saw it happening and we did hope you would too, and then Oscar and his coming here on his own and them going off together. Melanie feels terrible...'

'Oh, poor thing. There's no need, only I must be quite sure that she loves him and he loves her. What do you think, Mother?'

Mrs Rodner said simply, 'They saw each other and fell in love—not infatuation, dear, they can't help themselves. Did you feel like that with Oscar? A kind of blinding flash and you know you'll never be happy with anyone else.'

Megan had followed her back into the kitchen, freed Meredith and poured coffee for them both. Facing her mother across the table she said, 'No, Mother, I didn't feel like that—I was happy and content to be with Oscar and I thought life with him would be pleasant—he's such a good-natured man.'

'My dear child, love doesn't take into account good nature or being pleasant. A woman can fall in love with—and love deeply—a bad-tempered, impatient man who leaves towels all over the bathroom floor and forgets her birthday and still adores her.'

For a surprised moment Megan found herself wondering if the professor left towels all over the bathroom floor. 'I've got to make Melanie see that my heart isn't broken. It cracked a little but I know I shall get over it and it was a shock, but I've had time to get used to the idea and the sooner he and I call it off and he gets engaged and married to Melanie the better.'

'Does anyone know? At the hospital, I mean?'

Megan was annoyed with herself for blushing. 'Professor van Belfeld knows. He—he met me in one of the hospital corridors and wormed it out of me.'

Mrs Rodner gazed intently into her mug. 'I dare say he gave you some good advice,' she suggested.

'Well, yes, he did. He told me to do what I am doing—make sure that Melanie really loves Oscar.'

'What a sensible man, and very understanding. Married, I dare say, and with children of his own.'

'He never talks about himself but from one or two things he has said I think he must be.'

'Well, he's not a young man,' commented her mother.

'He's not all that old, forty at the outside.' Megan spoke quite sharply and her mother gave her a thoughtful glance, aware that her pretty daughter wasn't telling her everything. She still thought that the professor harboured an interest in Megan and of course there was always the danger that a man working for long weeks away from his home might fall in love with any pretty girl he met. She didn't believe that he was such a man. He could be a widower, of course, or she could be mistaken and he was merely giving advice to a colleague who seemed in need of it. He hadn't looked at Megan as though she were a colleague, though, he had looked at her as though he loved her. Mrs Rodner was quite sure about that. Moreover Megan had not the faintest idea . . .

She glanced at the clock. 'It's still early. Do you want to talk to Melanie right away? Because if you do you could go to meet her. Walking along together makes talking much easier than sitting facing each other in a room.'

Despite Megan's brave words, Mrs Rodner was worried to see her daughter's pale, drained face and the shadows under her eyes. The sooner things were sorted out, the better.

Megan got into a pair of old shoes, made sure that the cat was safely sleeping in the kitchen and went off in search of her sister.

Their mother was putting lunch on the table by the time they got back to the house, arm-in-arm. Megan was dry-eyed with a cheerful face which looked as though it might crack at any moment, but Melanie had wept buckets, although no amount of weeping could spoil her pretty little face. Mr Rodner had come in for his lunch but, well primed by his wife, made no comment, only greeted Megan with his usual affection and with his usual concern enquired after her work. 'I'm glad you're home,' he observed. 'The garden's in a shambles and I was hoping to get the sweet peas in and stake the beans. I'm going to try my hand at salsify, if I can get the seedlings transplanted, and I've some asparagus crowns, the ground is ready for planting...'

It was exactly what Megan wanted; she had had her talk with Melanie and now knew for certain that she loved Oscar and that he loved her but at the same time felt guilty about it. She managed to make Melanie understand that she had no need to feel any guilt. 'These things happen, love,' she had told her sobbing sister, 'but think how awful it would have been if you had discovered how much you loved each other after Oscar and I had got married. There's no harm done and my heart isn't broken, you see, I don't think I love—loved Oscar in the same way as you do and I shall get over it very quickly.' She had made her promise not to say anything to Oscar, though, not until she had had a chance to talk to him herself. She dreaded having to do that but in the meantime she could spend the weekend grubbing around in the garden, a soothing occupation which would do much to get her over an awkward few days. All the same, tired after her planting and weeding, she cried herself to sleep. Being cheerful when she wanted above all things to throw things around and scream loudly when her feelings got too much for her was quite exhausting.

Her mother and father made things as easy as possible for her; beyond listening quietly while she told them and observing that she was doing the right thing, they gave her no advice, nor did they overwhelm her with sympathy.

'An awkward situation which we shall get over,' her father had told her. 'These things happen. I'm only glad that it happened before you and Oscar got married or even had begun to talk seriously about it.'

Which, come to think of it, reflected Megan, they never had. They actually had settled down into a pleasant engagement with only the vaguest of vague mention of marrying. There had seemed no hurry; Oscar's future was all-important and she had realised that it might be some time before his mother was prepared to get to know her and even like her. She reminded herself of these facts several times a day and they dulled her hurt but didn't dispel the thought of an empty future.

Driving herself back on Sunday evening, she rehearsed what she would say to Oscar; she would be very calm and sensible and not let him see how humiliated she felt, and even when she had done that she would have to tell her friends at Regent's, and that wouldn't be easy. She was liked at the hospital, but, all the same, there would be a good deal of gossip. It wouldn't last long, thank heaven, and she would have to bear with it until some other interesting titbit of news crept into the grapevine.

Upon reflection she decided not to wait until Oscar rang her, as he did from time to time when he knew that he would have an hour to spare in the evening, so it wasn't until Tuesday at noon that the porter's lodge gave her a message to say that he was free after six that evening. 'No time for a meal,' his note read, 'but we might have a drink.'

Tuesday seemed endless. Not only was she longing for the evening, but the day was full of small mishaps—notes mislaid, X-Ray cancelling a barium meal, one of the student nurses cutting her hand on a glass she had broken... As she went off duty at last she found herself wishing that the wretched day could have gone on forever; all her carefully thought-out speeches had flown out of her head and she had the terrible feeling that she would burst into tears the moment she set eyes on Oscar's face. To make matters worse, she met the professor as she was leaving the hospital. He was coming in and held the door for her, planting himself in her path so that she was forced to stop.

'Off for the evening?' he enquired genially. 'Going to see young Fielding? Splendid.' He smiled at her and the smile was so kind that she wanted to throw herself on to his waistcoat and have a good cry. 'Now, now,' he said in his quiet voice, 'it won't be as bad as you think. You shall tell me all about it later on.'

She looked at him in astonishment. 'How did you know?'

'I do have access to the staff rota,' he pointed out. He patted her on the shoulder. 'Run along now, and get it over.'

He might have been talking to a little girl instead of a splendidly built young woman of eight and twenty.

Strangely enough she felt better; he had never criti-cised either Oscar or herself and his comments and advice had been impersonal and yet she felt comforted. She made a pot of tea, gave Meredith his supper and wasted a good deal of time deciding what to wear. Somehow it seemed important that she should be suitably dressed. She decided on a checked wool skirt, a shirt and a scarlet sweater to brighten up the black and white of the skirt and since it was a downcast evening she topped these with a black corduroy jacket. She would have liked to have worn something pretty and summery but the weather had turned, with all the suddenness of an English spring, into the chill of a damp February. At any rate, she decided, peering into the tiny looking-glass, the outfit was cheerful.

Oscar was waiting for her by the hospital gates. He took her arm and walked her across to the pub, ex-plaining that he could spare only half an hour as he sat her down at a table in the saloon bar. 'What is it to be?' he asked.

'Tonic, please.' She smiled at him, studying his face. Such a nice face, she thought. She was going to miss him even though they were bound to meet a good deal in the future, as much outside the hospital as inside. He looked worried and she supposed that he was.

'If you've only got half an hour there's something I want to say quickly so please don't interrupt,' she begged him. 'I know about you and Melanie... No, Oscar, I asked you not to interrupt. I've been home and talked about it with her and it's quite all right. I think that you loved me, but not enough, and you do love her, don't you?'

She sipped her tonic and wished that she had asked for something stronger.

She slid the ring off her finger and pushed it across the little table. 'I shall like having you for a brother-in-law and you don't have to feel guilty. It could have happened to anyone.'

'You, Megan, don't you mind—didn't you love me at all? I wanted to tell you but I didn't want to upset you. I thought that perhaps…I thought you would be broken-hearted.'

Megan felt a surge of impatience. 'Of course I mind and of course I loved you but not enough, I think, and as for being broken-hearted…my heart is cracked just a little.'

'Oh, Meg, I'm so very sorry. I should have told you straight away. The moment I set eyes on Melanie I knew. She's so beautiful and sweet. We plan to get married soon—I'll get a practice in the country. I'll have to buy a partnership…'

He really loved Melanie, thought Megan. He had given up his planned future without a sigh, he was going to do just what she herself had wanted him to do but for Melanie he was doing it gladly, without a backward glance at a consultant's post. Suddenly she couldn't stand any more. She left her tonic almost untouched and got to her feet. Somehow she managed a smile. 'I must fly— I'm going out. I'll see you around. Do phone Melanie as soon as you can. She worries so.'

She raced out of the pub and through the shabby streets to her flat and saw the Rolls parked outside it. The professor was lolling against the bonnet, talking to a group of small boys, but when he saw her he left them and was at her door to take the key from her and open it.

She didn't look at him. She was fighting back tears. 'Don't you dare to come in,' she said in a watery voice, and found herself gently urged inside, dumped in the chair and given Meredith to nurse.

'What you need is a nice cup of tea,' said the professor placidly. 'I have found that in this country people recover rapidly when offered a really strong brew, well milked and sugared.' He put on the kettle and began to whistle as he found cups and saucers and the teapot. 'This is, of course, only a temporary measure. When you've had your tea and a good cry, washed your face and tidied yourself, we will drive somewhere and have something to eat with a bottle of champagne.'

'Champagne?' wailed Megan. 'That's for celebrating. Oh, do go away!'

He took no notice, merely offered her a large white handkerchief and warmed the teapot, made the tea and brought the tray to the table beside her chair. He poured the tea and put it by her. 'Drink it while it is hot, only stop crying for a moment while you do so.'

Megan sniffed. 'I don't want any tea...'

'Tut-tut, that's no way to talk. Did you howl all over young Fielding?'

She blew her nose. 'Of course I didn't.' She added indignantly between sniffs, 'I do think I might be left alone to cry if I want to.'

He reached out and took the hanky from her and mopped her face. 'Drink your tea. No need to cry any more, it's over and done with.' Then when she obediently sipped, he added, 'That's the girl. Had you thought? Until this evening there were three unhappy people, but now there is only one.'

She drank some more tea. She said in a small voice, 'You're very kind. I'm sorry I'm so cross and rude.'

'Think nothing of it. Finish your tea, wash your face and we'll go out. I'm hungry.'

'I can't—I must look a fright.'

'A very beautiful fright. A comb run through your hair and a touch of powder on the nose and you'll be even more beautiful.'

She got up and went to the mirror in the kitchen; she looked a positive hag. Besides, she had had a disquieting thought.

'It's very kind of you to ask me to go out with you but I don't think that I should. Wouldn't your—your wife object?'

He had been rubbing a delighted Meredith's ears. Now he gave her a kindly impersonal glance. 'I am quite sure that my wife would not object.' He spoke casually.

She was holding a cold cloth to her eyes. 'You don't think I'm being silly and old-fashioned?'

'Not in the least. I'm old-fashioned myself.'

Satisfied, Megan squeezed into the shower-room and washed her face, feeling better. 'I'll have to do my hair and face in the kitchen, if you don't mind.'

'Not in the least.' He had sat down in the armchair with Meredith on his lap and was leafing through a book he had taken from the shelves.

It was surprising, she reflected, doing things to her face, that, despite the size of him, he contrived to be so self-effacing.

'Will I do as I am?' she asked him, very neat once more, her beautiful nose only faintly pink now.

'Admirably. We aren't going anywhere grand.'

He took her to Datchet, taking the M4 out of London and turning off just before they reached Windsor. The hotel overlooked the village green and she saw with relief that it was a quiet country restaurant where her clothes would go unremarked. The professor had chosen well. There was a fairly full dining-room with plenty of people dining but they were quiet and the tables were well spaced. He gave her a drink in the bar before they were led to a table in one of the windows. They studied their menus for a moment before he asked, 'Is there anything that you would particularly like?'

When she shook her head he said, 'Shall we have salade Niçoise to start with? The roast duck with oranges and Curaçao is very good here...'

'You have been here?'

'It's very convenient for Heathrow,' he told her. 'Braised chicory and sauté potatoes?' He gave their order and began an easygoing conversation until the salad arrived and with it the champagne, and throughout the meal he didn't allow the talk to verge even for a moment on anything but the lightest of topics. Megan, eating peaches poached in syrup, felt almost guiltily content. As they drank their coffee he asked her if she was on duty in the morning and when she said yes he said briskly, 'In that case we should be getting back. You need a good night's sleep.'

If she had an elder brother, she reflected, he would sound just like that, and of course, she reminded herself, he had taken her out because he was a kind man and she had been upset. He would have done that for anyone, not because he particularly wished for her company.

She went out to the car with him, a little muzzy from the champagne, and sat silently beside him as he drove back to the flat where he got out and opened her door and held out a hand for the door key, going in first and looking around him before cutting short her thanks in the nicest possible manner and driving himself away. He wasn't a man to waste time over the meaningless conversation which so often followed such an occasion; she just had time to say thank you and no more than that.

'Well, as I thought,' she told Meredith, 'it wasn't as if he invited me out because he wanted to. I dare say he won't speak to me for days.'

The cat yawned and climbed on to the divan and went instantly to sleep although, later, when he heard Megan crying very softly, he crept up to her and curled up against her shoulder, muttering gently into her ear.

She was quite right; she didn't see the professor for several days, but she did see Oscar, who greeted her in a shamefaced fashion which caused her to beg him not to be silly. The hospital knew all about it by now and she was aware that there was a good deal of gossip, but her friends rallied round, inviting themselves for supper when she was off duty in the evening, suggesting window-shopping if they were free in the afternoons, and presently the gossip died down and even Oscar managed to behave quite normally if they happened to meet, something which was inevitable. She still felt sad and lost but there was no denying that Oscar was happy, and Melanie when she phoned bubbled over with happiness. In a month or so, Megan told herself, she would appreciate the wisdom of her action, although for the moment she found herself dwelling on what might have been rather too frequently.

She didn't allow her feelings to interfere with her work; she presented a calm face to her nurses and patients and beyond Jenny's quietly voiced regret nothing had been said, even Mr Bright, usually so outspoken, refrained from more than a muttered, 'Sorry to hear about you and young Fielding, Megan,' as he finished his round. It seemed that there was a quiet conspiracy to bury the whole unhappy business, or so she thought until going on duty one morning she encountered the professor sauntering into the hospital. He wished her good morning and asked cheerfully, 'Seen anything of young Fielding? I dare say it is a bit awkward at first but one gets used to anything in time.' He had, as he often did, stopped in front of her so that she couldn't pass him easily, not without giving him a push in the waistcoat.

She wished him good morning rather coldly. Why did he have to start the day off badly just as she was getting over the whole affair? Since it was obvious that he was waiting for an answer she said, 'Yes, I've seen Oscar several times. He and Melanie are very happy, and I am happy too.' She lifted her chin at him and was annoyed by his smile.

'Now that is good news; you're far too young to become embittered. It's a good thing to fall in and out of love several times so that when it is the real thing you are aware of the difference. Just like young Fielding.'

'You're being very nasty,' said Megan. 'I know you're a consultant and I'm supposed to respect you but I'm not on duty yet and neither are you.'

'Ah, that's the spirit. Get it off that delightful chest of yours, Meg. I'll drive you home on your day off and you can show your family how well you've recovered.'

She drew a deep breath. 'I don't want——' she began crossly.

'Friday, isn't it? I'll be outside your flat at half-past eight. Mind you're ready.'

'Well, I won't be,' said Megan, shaking with temper. She managed to edge past him and flew through the hospital to her ward. He had made her late and put her into a frightful temper besides.

She took the night nurse's report with a slightly heightened colour and the night staff nurse had to repeat a remark twice, something which had never happened before. When they had gone and Jenny was sitting opposite her at the desk while they conned the day's work, she so far forgot herself as to draw squiggles all over her clean blotting-paper pad while her trusty aide tried in vain to interest her in Mrs Briggs' grumbles about her breakfast. She caught Jenny's eye and smiled reluctantly, 'Sorry, Jenny, I'm a bit put out. What's this about Mrs Briggs? She tends to be tiresome, doesn't she? Supposing we move her bed to the other side of the ward before she starts annoying old Mrs Coke beside her?' She turned the blotting paper over. 'Now, who shall we send to Theatre with the first case?'

CHAPTER FIVE

MEGAN told herself several times that she had no intention of driving down with the professor on Friday but all the same she found herself burrowing through her wardrobe, intent on looking her best. The little grey jacket and the pleated skirt would do; she did look nice in it, it was elegant and it suited her. She put it ready for the morning and went to bed and got up half an hour later to put it back in the cupboard and fish around for a corduroy skirt in peat-brown, a rust-coloured silk shirt and a brown cardigan with a shawl collar. She intended to go walking when she got home as well as pottering in the garden; it would be silly to dress up. Sudden tears crowded her throat. There was no point in dressing up, for there was no one to dress up for. She got back into bed and presently fell into a fitful sleep. A pity, for when she got up in the morning she hardly looked her best, so that, despite her best efforts, when she opened the door to the professor's thunderous knock the first thing he said was, 'You've been moping again. A good thing that you have a day at home.' He picked up Meredith, snarling quietly in his basket, and ushered her out of her door and into the car, put Meredith on the back seat and got in beside her. Without looking at her he said, 'We'll go the long way round, shall we? What time are you expected home?'

'When I drive myself I usually get there about eleven o'clock.'

87

'Good. We'll go through High Wycombe and then turn off. That will give you time to tell me why you look so down-in-the-mouth.'

'I'm nothing of the sort, Professor, merely a little tired.'

'If that is what you want to call it—so why are you a little tired?' He gave her a quick glance. 'Ward too much for you?'

'Of course not,' she snapped. 'I took it over nearly five years ago...'

'You're in a rut—you need a change.'

'Are you being tactful and telling me that now that Oscar and I aren't going to be married it would be a good idea if I left Regent's?' Her voice had become a little shrill.

'Certainly not. You are a good ward sister—and I for one would be very sorry to see you go.'

'But you've just suggested...'

'That you should leave? Yes.' He hadn't raised his voice, but he almost never did. 'However, that is a matter for you to decide, isn't it? As long as you see Oscar—and you can't avoid that, can you?—you will brood and mope, not because you're in love with him but because you are raking over old ashes, and that, Megan, is a waste of time.'

Megan fumed silently. She hated to admit it, but he was right, although it meant that she would have to give up her job—hers for the rest of her life, she imagined, and start all over again, away from London, she supposed, somewhere where she wouldn't see Oscar more than occasionally. She began to go over in her mind the possibilities of a move but she was interrupted almost at once by her companion. 'Forget it,' he told her quietly.

'Enjoy your day. I'm going to turn off and take some inside roads. What are you going to do with yourself?'

'Garden, go for a walk with Melanie, I expect, eat too much.'

They were driving along a country road with trees on either side and fields beyond, the sky was blue but there was a brisk wind and clouds tumbling along the horizon. 'Good weather for walking,' said the professor, 'and it won't hurt you to eat too much. You've lost weight.'

Megan blushed and thought how silly she was to do that. His tone had been quite impersonal—the voice any medical man would use towards a patient. She looked out of the window and didn't see his quick glance and little smile.

They reached her home at half-past ten. She hadn't let her mother know that the professor was bringing her, obstinately certain until the last minute that she wouldn't go with him, but Mrs Rodner showed no surprise at the sight of the car. She came out of the house to meet them, hugged her daughter and turned to the professor. 'How nice to see you again, and this time you must stay for coffee.'

She led the way into the house. 'You surely don't have to go straight back?'

He smiled down at her. 'No, Mrs Rodner.'

'Splendid, stay for lunch. Megan can take you for a good walk before tea. I don't suppose it takes you long to get back to London in that car of yours?'

He glanced at Megan, standing silent. 'If we leave here by eight o'clock we can be at Regent's by Megan's bedtime. But I came unexpectedly; you may have to do something else. I had intended to come back for Megan this evening.'

'Nonsense—a day in the country will do you a great deal of good—unless you have something better to do in London?'

Her tone implied that there was nothing better to do there.

'You're very kind, but what has Megan to say to that?'

She had been well brought up and her manners were nice, so she said now, 'I'm sure that a quiet day here will do the professor good.' She looked at him then. 'It's very kind of you to drive me back this evening.'

Mrs Rodner, bustling out to the kitchen to fetch the coffee, smiled to herself.

'Where's Melanie?' asked Megan presently. They were in the drawing-room, the rather thin sunlight streaming in through the old-fashioned french windows.

'Friday, dear,' reminded her mother, 'doing the flowers at the church. She'll be back as soon as she can. I did tell you that she and Oscar are going to see his parents next weekend?'

Megan went a little pale but her voice was steady. 'I do hope Mrs Fielding likes her, though I don't see how she could help herself. Does Melanie want to spend the night before they go?'

'I believe that Oscar's worked out an easy route from here—he'll collect her on the way.' Her mother turned to the professor. 'Do you like living in England, Professor? Your English is so perfect I keep forgetting that you're Dutch. Do you go home often?'

'Oh, frequently. I'm fond of the country here, though, and I've spent a good deal of time here and it's so easy to go to and fro.'

'Are you a pathologist there as well?'

'Yes, in a consultant capacity just as I am at Regent's.'

'You must lead a busy life.' She looked at Megan. 'Megan leads a busy life too, too busy I sometimes think. She needs a change.'

Megan choked over her coffee. Two people within a couple of hours wanting her to alter her life; it just needs one more, reflected Megan, and I might be convinced.

Mrs Rodner got up. 'Well, my dears, I'm going to see to lunch. No, Meg, I don't want any help but you could go down to the village and see if Mrs Slocombe has got any of those nice cheese biscuits, and you might collect Melanie on the way back.'

At the door she paused. 'Take the professor with you, Meg; he may like to see the village.'

'Perhaps you'd rather sit in the garden,' suggested Megan.

Sounding his most bland, the professor pointed out that he had been sitting in the car all morning. 'Exercise will be good for both of us,' he observed in a reasonable voice which she suspected hid amusement.

The village was ten minutes' walk away, a pretty walk along a leafy lane with fields on either side of it, alive with sheep and their lambs.

'Delightful,' commented the professor, standing still and taking deep breaths into his massive chest. 'Have you no dog?'

'Janus—he's with Father. Melanie wants a puppy but if she is to be married soon she would want to take it with her. Mother would like one but she thought she had better wait until Melanie has gone.'

'What kind of a dog?' he asked idly.

'We had a spaniel. She was a darling, we called her Flossy, but it had better be another kind so as not to remind us too much of her.'

'Of course.' They had reached the village, crossed the green and stopped outside Mrs Slocombe's shop. It was the post office as well and served as an information centre concerning the gossip, scandal and goings-on in the village. 'I dare say you'd rather wait outside,' said Megan, knowing that the sight of them together would give the village a chance to freshen up the various rumours going around about her engagement to Oscar being at an end. However, he took no notice, despite the fact that the shop was fairly full. He opened the door and its old-fashioned bell announced their arrival to several pairs of sharp ears and eyes.

There was a chorus of good-mornings while the professor was thoroughly looked over. 'On holiday, Miss Megan?' asked Mrs Slocombe, abandoning her weighing of a pound of prunes for the wife of the gardener up at the Manor House.

'No, no, Mrs Slocombe, just a day off.'

'Brought a friend with you, have you, love?'

'Someone from the hospital has been kind enough to give me a lift.'

Mrs Slocombe finished with the prunes. 'That's nice,' she commented, and the ladies in the shop murmured a chorus of agreement, still staring at the professor, who stood smiling at everyone, completely at his ease.

'Happen you're in a bit of a hurry, Miss Megan, seeing as it's only a day, like. I'm sure Mrs Thomson won't mind if I serve you right away.'

'That's very kind. Mother wondered if you had any of those cheese biscuits she usually has.' Megan flushed a little and the flush deepened when she heard the professor replying to Mrs Thomson's remark about the lovely spring they were having. She knew it wouldn't stop there and it didn't; Mrs Thomson enquired archly where he came from, and, when he said placidly, 'I'm from Holland,' drew in her breath with a hiss of interest everyone else could hear.

'Fancy that, now; just on a visit, I dare say?'

He assured her in equable tones that he lived in London for a good deal of the year. 'Well, I never,' declared Mrs Thomson. 'So of course you know our Miss Megan.'

'Indeed I do.'

'Staying for lunch, I dare say,' said the nosy lady. 'Came in a car, I expect.'

'Yes. This village is off the beaten track, is it not? Such a charming place.'

Mrs Slocombe had taken as long as possible to find the biscuits and put them in a bag; she took even longer to give Megan her change.

Megan thanked her politely, wished everyone there good day and was ushered out of the shop by an attentive professor. The door wasn't quite closed when she heard the spate of gossip.

'I did ask you if you wanted to stay outside,' she said crossly. 'It's only a very small village and everyone knows everyone else's business and makes up the rest.'

'But we have nothing to hide,' he pointed out blandly, and took the biscuits from her, put a hand under her elbow and steered her towards the church.

'That isn't what I meant,' snapped Megan, and when he laughed softly she said, 'Oh, do be serious...'

He stopped in the middle of the green, in full view of anyone who might be watching them. 'My dear Megan, don't be peevish and spoil my day. So far I have enjoyed every minute of it.'

She wouldn't look at him but marched into the church with her head held so high that she didn't look where she was going and tripped over a heap of greenery. The professor set her back on her feet with an infuriating, 'Tut, tut,' and remarked, 'There is Melanie. Do you suppose that she is ready?'

There was no need to answer him, for she came dancing towards them, not minding the various people, including the vicar's wife, who turned to stare at the newcomers. Her brow cleared when she saw Megan and she came down the aisle at a decorous pace, the expression on her face indicative of sympathy and curiosity.

'My dear Megan,' she began before Melanie could say hello, 'I was shocked to hear your news.' She glanced at Melanie's red face and added hastily, 'Although as the vicar said to me it is an ill wind which blows no good; I'm sure that we all hope Melanie will be very happy.'

She looked at the professor. 'Your mother has a friend staying?'

'Just someone who gave me a lift home,' said Megan airily. 'You don't mind if I take Melanie away? We're lunching early. Goodbye, Mrs Brewster.'

She smiled with charm and plucked her sister on the arm before anyone could say anything more. 'I'm only here for the day, so you'll excuse us if we don't stop.'

They were out of sight of the church before she looked at the professor. He was smiling. 'I should have introduced you,' she apologised, 'but if I had it would have been a bit difficult...you do see?'

He had tucked an arm into Melanie's as they strolled along. His shoulders shook. 'You could have introduced me as an uncle or old friend of your father.'

'You're not nearly old enough,' Megan pointed out, 'though I suppose at a pinch...'

It was Melanie who cried, 'Megan, how could you suggest that? The professor's quite young.' She looked up at him. 'You are, aren't you?'

'Shall we say youngish? Melanie, you are a girl after my own heart; you haven't even noticed my grey hairs.'

She began to laugh and he teased her gently all the way home. They were crossing the garden when Melanie said, 'Meg, I'm going to stay with Oscar's parents...'

'Yes, love, I know; Mother told me. Mrs Fielding didn't like me, but I'm sure she'll like you, and you'll be able to twist Oscar's father round your thumb.'

Melanie stopped to look at her. 'You're the nicest sister. You look a bit pale, though, and tired. You need a change. Why don't you leave that old hospital of yours and do something different?'

Megan said a bit wildly, 'Look, darling, you're the third person who's told me to uproot myself. You don't mean it, do you?'

Melanie didn't answer because her mother came to meet them.

'Did you get the biscuits? Good. What do you think of our village, Professor?'

'Delightful, and such friendly inhabitants.'

Megan shot him a glance, but his handsome face bore no other expression than one of calm pleasure.

'They are nosy,' said Melanie. 'Mrs Brewster was in the church...I shall be cross-examined next time I see her, but I shan't answer.' Which for Melanie was an unwontedly fiery remark. 'Of course it's because you are so large.' She smiled at the professor with none of her usual shyness and Megan stared in surprise and pleasure. He might be a tiresome man but he knew how to put Melanie at ease, and yet at the hospital the junior nurses, even some of the staff nurses, would do anything to avoid him.

They all went into the house and since they were having a lively conversation about village life she was able to continue her musing. He was a brilliantly clever man, and she suspected that when he was working nothing but perfection satisfied him; clumsiness, carelessness and incompetence would be bound to make him angry, the cold anger so well controlled but just the same intimidating. She nodded her head in satisfaction at having solved her problem and looked up to find him gazing at her. He couldn't possibly have known what she was thinking about but she went pink all the same so that he smiled faintly.

Her father came home for lunch, which they ate in the rather shabby dining-room with its heavy, well polished furniture. Mrs Rodner, put on her mettle by her unexpected guest, had surpassed herself. Steak and kidney pudding wrapped in a white napkin, creamed potatoes light as feathers, spinach and the first baby carrots from the garden, followed by apple pie and cream. 'The last of the Bramleys,' she told her companions, beaming at the professor when he remarked upon the mouth-watering pastry. 'Oh, good, I'm glad you're enjoying it—it's not really very cordon bleu, I'm afraid. Megan has a much lighter hand with pastry than I have.'

They all looked at Megan, who mumbled something and got up to clear the plates and fetch the cheese and biscuits. The professor had made a good lunch; he and her father got on well although the talk was general and not at all serious, and when they had finished their coffee Mr Rodner got up reluctantly.

'I must get back to the office—you will be here when I get home soon after five o'clock?'

'We shan't need to leave before eight o'clock. Your wife has very kindly asked me to stay for supper.'

'Splendid. We may have time to examine some rather fine prints I have of this part of the world.' He patted Megan on the shoulder. 'This is just what you need, my dear. You are far too pale and surely you have lost some weight? It won't do, you know. You need to get away from the hospital—a change of scene . . .' He caught his wife's eye and added hastily, 'Well, I must be off. Enjoy your afternoon.'

To Megan's surprise she did enjoy her afternoon. The professor expressed a wish to see something of the countryside and since Janus had stayed home they had taken him with them. 'He still misses Flossy,' said Megan, leading the way along a bridlepath towards the woods ahead of them. 'This is Nib's Wood,' she told him as they entered its tangled green and waited patiently while Janus explored a rabbit hole, and the professor looked around him and observed in a voice so quiet that she almost didn't hear what he had said, 'Where you came with Oscar, no doubt.'

Remembering that, she felt that she should have been upset but although she had a pang of regret she answered him quite naturally. 'It's a lovely spot, isn't it?'

They walked for miles and got back home to eat a splendid tea of scones and jam and cream and a lovely buttery Madeira cake. 'Supper at half-past seven sharp,' said her mother as they got up from the table. 'It won't be much since you'll have to leave directly afterwards.'

'I feel that I should sing for my supper,' remarked the professor. 'Is there any digging to be done? If your suppers are anything like your lunches then I need to work up an appetite.'

Mrs Rodner laughed. 'You would like that? Really? Then get a spade from the shed. Megan will show you, there's a patch in the kitchen garden that needs double-digging for the asparagus. It's hard work—are you quite sure?'

He took off his jacket and rolled up his sleeves. 'A nice change from sitting at a desk or peering down a microscope,' he told her. 'Come along, Megan.'

She found him a spade. 'You'll ruin those trousers,' she pointed out.

'I do have another pair. Come and talk to me while I work.'

'Better still, I'll weed the carrots.' She donned a pair of gardening gloves and set to with a vengeance, watching him out of the corner of her eye.

He was working with an effortless ease and with breath left to talk. A gentle, rambling conversation which exactly suited their peaceful surroundings, the rumble of his quiet voice and the sound of the spade sliding in and out of the earth with the regularity of a ticking clock coupled with the weeding giving her a feeling of content she hadn't experienced since she had broken up with Oscar. Her father came to talk to them presently and joined in the chat, sitting on an old wheelbarrow, smoking his pipe, well content to see someone else doing the hard work. The digging was half done by the time they were called in to have supper and as he helped Megan stow the tools away the professor sighed. 'A splendid relaxation.' He glanced at Megan's nicely pink cheeks. 'We both needed it.'

She went ahead of the two men to wash and tidy herself and Melanie followed her up to her bedroom. 'He's nice, your professor,' she remarked, sitting on the bed watching Megan brush out her tangled hair.

'He's not mine, love, and when we get back to Regent's he will very likely ignore me if we should chance to meet. Besides, he has a wife, you know.'

'How funny—I mean, he doesn't seem like a married man, does he?' She got off the bed and came to peer over Meg's shoulder into the looking glass. 'I do hope Oscar's mother and father will like me...'

'They will, darling, I'm quite sure of that. You see, Oscar really loves you and they will see that and love you too.'

'Is that why Mrs Fielding didn't like you?'

Megan powdered her nose. 'Yes, I do like to think that it was.'

'You're not unhappy, Megan?'

'No, love, I promise you that.' She smiled at her sister's anxious reflection.

'Oh, good. Oscar and I wouldn't like that. I still think it would be nice if you were to change your job. See the world, meet people...'

Megan laughed. 'Why, Melanie, you sound motherly! Perhaps I will. I'll see.'

They went downstairs and found everyone in the drawing-room, drinking her father's best sherry, the professor looking completely at home.

They left promptly at eight o'clock after their supper of cheese soufflé and jacket potatoes, which, thanks to their gardening, they had eaten with splendid appetites. Megan had never felt so reluctant to leave home and neither had Meredith, judging by the grumbling voice issuing from his basket. They didn't talk much; there didn't seem to be any need for small talk. She sat, full of fresh air and good food, half asleep, and the professor made no effort to rouse her. There was very little traffic and this time he used the motorway, only slowing down as they reached the outskirts of the city. She roused herself then but since her one or two remarks were met with monosyllabic replies she lapsed into silence until he stopped before the flat. The street looked gloomy and drab and the flat even worse. She got out when he opened her door and took her key and admitted himself to turn on the lights and look around him. She had followed him in and stood in the little room while he fetched Meredith.

'Would you like a cup of tea—or coffee?' She let the cat out of his basket. 'Thank you very much for taking me home and bringing me back. It was a lovely day.'

He stood looking at her. He nodded and said to surprise her, 'You're still not quite cured, are you? Sleep well, Megan.' At the door he turned. 'I too found it a lovely day. Goodnight.'

She didn't see him for the next few days and then it was a brief visit in response to Mr Bright's urgent request that he should confer with him on the ward. He came into the ward silently, his white coat open, its pockets bulging with papers. He looked remote and meeting his cold eyes and responding politely to his distant, 'Good morning, Sister,' Megan quite understood why the nurses held him in awe; it was hard to reconcile him with the man who had stood in Mrs Slocombe's shop meekly answering Mrs Thomson's questions.

She did see a lot of Oscar, though. Now that he had got over the initial awkwardness of breaking off their engagement he waylaid her whenever he could and talked about Melanie, delegating her to the role of future sister-in-law willing to listen to his plans for the future and Melanie's perfection. Megan agreed with him; Melanie was a darling, and to see her happy made Megan happy too, but she found it wearing listening to plans which she and Oscar might have been making for their own future. Not that she wished to marry him; indeed, she realised now that what she had felt for him had been only a strong attraction and a deep affection. She still had the affection for he was a man willing to like everyone, with an even temper and good-natured. Just right for Melanie. She began to think that it wasn't such a bad idea to find another job. Make a clean break and start again, she told Meredith as she let herself into her flat after meeting Oscar as she was going off duty and listening to his account of the weekend he and Melanie had enjoyed at his parents' home. Melanie had been a great success, he told her with pride.

'Which is more than I was,' said Megan, addressing Meredith once again since there was no one else to talk to. 'In fact I don't think I'm a success with anyone.'

Meredith, gobbling his supper, took no notice, but he lifted his head when the door-knocker was thumped and Megan, her head inside the small kitchen cupboard, deciding what she would have for her supper, withdrew it rapidly and went to answer it. It was no good looking out of the window, for, being a basement, it afforded her a view of feet and not much else, but the knock had sounded urgent; it would be someone from the hospital, she supposed, although they could have phoned her— one of her friends at a loose end and wanting supper. She opened the door and found the professor blocking the daylight.

'Oh,' said Megan, and then, 'Good evening, Professor.'

'I wish to talk to you,' he glanced round him, 'but not here. Perhaps you would come with me and I will give you a meal.'

'What about?'

'If you will come with me I will tell you.'

She could hear impatience in his quiet voice; all the same she persisted, 'I was just about to get my supper.'

He went past her and looked into the alcove she called the kitchen. His raised eyebrows questioned the lack of any food. 'I was getting it out of the cupboard,' said Megan snappishly, 'and why I should have to explain all this to you I really don't know.'

He said mildly, 'You will do very well as you are; just get a jacket. We aren't going far.'

'I don't...' She caught his eye and mumbled, 'Oh, well, if you insist. Has something awful happened at the hospital? I sent up all the specimens you wanted.'

'If it had been something to do with your work or your ward I would have seen you at the hospital.'

He wasn't going to budge. She got her jacket, advised Meredith to be a good boy and then said quietly, 'I'm ready.'

He ushered her out, locked the door and stowed her neatly into the car, waved politely to the various heads peering from neighbouring windows and drove off, into the Mile End Road, through the city and the King's Road, over Putney Bridge and so into Richmond.

'Why have you brought me here?' asked Megan. They had hardly spoken during the journey; the professor had been friendly enough but deep in thought and she hadn't minded, she had plenty to think about herself.

'I live here.' He had turned away from the main streets and was driving along a quiet road with large terraced houses overlooking the river. He stopped at the end house, got out and opened her door and invited her to get out too. He did it with a calm air but he said nothing more and she paused on the pavement to ask, 'Why didn't you tell me? Is it a secret or something?'

'I suspect that if I had told you I was taking you to my house you might have refused to come.'

'You're quite right.'

He smiled, 'You see?' He put a hand on her elbow. 'Shall we go in? I'm hungry—I hope you are too.'

He opened the door and ushered her into a small vestibule and at the same time the inner door was opened by a stout little man with a fringe of white hair and small twinkly eyes. He was dressed neatly in a black jacket and striped trousers and bade the professor good evening before bowing to Megan and repeating his greeting in a dignified voice.

'This is Thrumble,' said the professor. 'He and his wife look after me. Miss Rodner has come for dinner, Thrumble, tell Mrs Thrumble and take Miss Rodner's jacket if you please.'

Megan cast the professor a reproachful look. It was bad enough being whisked away at a moment's notice; it was even worse to find oneself in an elderly cotton top and a jersey skirt she kept strictly for evenings at home. She would have looked delightful in a paper bag, but even if anyone had told her so it would have been cold comfort.

An arm under her elbow, the professor urged her across the hall and into a room with vast windows overlooking the river. It was furnished with beautifully polished cabinets along one wall, a magnificent long-case clock in one corner, a rosewood sofa table behind a vast sofa upholstered in plum-coloured velvet and a very beautiful mahogany rent table between the windows, which were curtained in plum-coloured brocade, and here and there there were tripod tables with a lamp each, arranged beside comfortable armchairs.

Megan took it all in slowly. 'You don't live here, do you?' She blushed because it was a silly question. 'What I mean is—all alone?' Which was even worse.

The professor offered her a chair and went to the fireplace and stirred the logs in it with an elegant and extremely large foot. There was a tabby cat sitting before the fire and he bent and stroked it.

'Yes, I live here alone—except for the excellent Thrumbles. I inherited the house a long time ago and when I'm in England I live here. It is too large, I must admit, but that can be easily remedied.'

'Oh, of course, when your wife and children live here.' She was conscious that that troubled her.

'As you say, when my wife and children live here.'

He sat down in an armchair near her and she said matter-of-factly, 'You wanted to talk to me about something.'

'Yes. You need to get away, Megan, you know that, don't you? I think that I can help you. I am on the board of an orphanage in Holland, forty children, boys and girls between the ages of three months and twelve years...' She opened her mouth to speak and he lifted a large, well kept hand. 'No, let me finish. It is well staffed but one of the girls is going to Canada in a fortnight's time to visit her family; she will be gone for six weeks or so and her place will need to be filled—something you could do quite competently while you decide what you want to do next.'

'I don't speak or understand a word of Dutch.'

'Babies respond to any language and toddlers too, and all the staff know enough English for you to get by. The salary is less than you are getting at Regent's but the orphanage is very quietly situated—you would have little to spend your money upon—it's north of Amsterdam, on the coast. A small village near the seaside town of Castricum. The older children go to the village school but you would have most to do with the infants and toddlers. You would get normal off-duty hours but only one day a week and as I said the job is for six weeks or so.' He got up. 'Think about it while I get you a drink—sherry?'

She accepted the glass he offered. 'I can't make up my mind at the drop of a hat. In any case, I'm not sure that it is a good idea. Besides, you've taken me by surprise.'

'I intended to. Have you had a busy day on the ward?'

She said that yes she had and added, 'And what am I supposed to do when the six weeks is up?'

'I have always thought that it is best to cross one's bridges when one comes to them. Ah, here is Thrumble to tell us that dinner is ready.'

He ushered her out of the room and across the hall into another smaller room, also overlooking the river. It was handsomely furnished with a round mahogany table capable of seating eight persons. The chairs were mahogany too, as was the sideboard which took up almost all of one wall. The walls were hung with pale green silk and there were a great many gilt-framed pictures on the walls. The curtains were of a darker green velvet lined with dark red and tied back with red cords which matched the carpet exactly. Megan thoroughly approved of the room, just as she admired the white damask on the table and the shining silver and glass.

Mrs Thrumble was an excellent cook. She served up watercress soup, grilled sole and castle puddings with a wine sauce, and since Megan was hungry she did justice to all of these while maintaining a conversation about this and that which had nothing to do with the professor's surprising offer, and he for his part made no mention of it. Tiresome man, she reflected as she poured the coffee in the drawing-room; she supposed that she would have to bring the subject up. She was going to refuse, of course...

He cut across her thoughts. 'Have you any leave due to you?'

'Well, yes, about three weeks—I had to cancel a week in February because Jenny was ill and we were busy. I'm to have it added on to the two weeks I'm due.'

'Which means that you can leave at the end of a week.'

'Who said that I was going to leave?' snapped Megan.

'I did, because you know that that is what you want to do, only you're afraid to do it—to leave your comfortable rut and try your hand at something new.'

He smiled as he spoke and she had an urge to fling herself at him and pour out all her worries and woes. She said hesitantly, 'Do you really think that it's a good idea?'

'I wouldn't have suggested it unless I thought that, but you must make up your own mind, Megan.'

'I need to know a whole lot more about the job,' she told him.

'Of course. Pour us both more coffee and I will tell you.'

He had all the details at his fingertips and a satisfactory answer to all her questions. It might be a good idea, she mused, and no less than four people had told her that she should leave Regent's...

'Meredith,' she said suddenly.

'Your parents might look after him? Or, if not, he could be absorbed into this household without any

'It takes seconds only to say yes or no,' he sounded quite mild.

She said yes in a cross voice and the moment after wished she hadn't. It was most unfair of him to rush her like that... 'I shall come and see you this evening,' he said, and put the phone down.

She sailed down the ward to where Mr Bright was waiting, her colour high, her dark eyes flashing. Mr Bright looked at her over his glasses. 'Have you been rubbed up the wrong way? Are the reports not available yet?'

'They are being sent down now, sir, and there is nothing the matter, thank you.'

'A flash of temper suits you, Megan,' observed Mr Bright, and Megan, whose warm cheeks had begun to cool, pinkened again under the eyes of the registrar and the house surgeon. Men! thought Megan, becoming all at once the efficient, professional ward sister.

The round over and Mr Bright speeded on his way with his various assistants, she went into her office and sat down. There were ten minutes or so before the dinner trolleys would arrive; she could start on the next fort-night's off-duty list. She picked up her pen and put it down; the wretched man was coming that evening and she would have to offer him coffee at least. She had eaten the last of the biscuits, too. She had planned a salad for her supper and there was ham in the fridge—a good thing too, for she had no idea at what time he would arrive and with a cold meal she could have it ready in a few minutes once he had gone. She had done nothing about the off-duty list when Jenny came to warn her that dinners were ready to serve.

Jenny was off duty that afternoon. Megan asked, 'Are you going out, Jenny?' and, when she said yes, asked,

'Will you buy me some biscuits? I haven't a single one left and the shop's always so crowded by the time I get to it. Anything will do—rich tea or digestive.'

'Entertaining?' asked Jenny.

Megan was adjusting her cap in front of the looking glass and didn't look at her. 'Hardly, with biscuits like that, but people do pop in sometimes for a cup of coffee and you can be sure that they'll come when I've not a crumb to give them.' She went into the ward, served the dinners and then went to her own meal, where she joined in a discussion about the newest fashions with such light-heartedness that her friends there came to the conclusion that she had made a good recovery from Oscar.

'Although,' said one of them after she had gone back to her ward, 'Megan looked as though she was—well, excited about something.'

Megan, on the other hand was resolutely refusing to be excited; she had, she considered, been bullied into accepting a job she didn't want. If she left Regent's then it would be to another job as good as, or better than, the one she had now. She would tell the professor so when he came that evening. She was too busy to think up any suitable speeches during the afternoon but as she went off duty, armed with the rich tea biscuits, she tried out several beautifully worded refusals. At home, attending to the cat's wants while the kettle boiled for a cup of tea, she practised them out loud. She would take care to remain calm and polite and remember to thank him for his interest and she would offer him a cup of coffee and one of the biscuits. Having got her plans nicely sorted out, she put the cups and saucers ready on a tray, put a saucepan of milk ready on the cooker and arranged the biscuits on a plate. She ate two of them with her tea; supper might be hours away.

She tidied away her teacup, did her hair and her face and, since there was no sign of him, began to wash her smalls in the sink. If he had left the hospital at his usual time he would have been at the door by now; probably he had gone home first to eat a delicious meal. The very thought made her feel hungry and she ate another biscuit. Her mouth was full and her hands were covered in soapy water when the knocker was thumped. She snatched up a towel and went to the door, drying her hands as she went, anxious to admit him before the neighbours got to their windows.

She opened the door, wished him good evening through the biscuit and finished drying her hands. 'Will the car be all right?' she wanted to know. He moved a little to one side so that she could see round him; there were four little boys sitting in it like statues.

'It's in good hands,' he told her casually. 'Were you not expecting me?'

She felt at a disadvantage. 'Of course I was but you didn't say when you were coming and I do have chores to do; you're late, anyway.'

He didn't answer that but his eyes gleamed beneath their lids as she lifted Meredith off the easy-chair. 'Do sit down. Would you like a cup of coffee?'

'Indeed I should.' He took the cat from her and settled him on his knees, 'What a splendid chap Meredith has become.'

She put on the milk and spooned instant coffee and agreed while she debated whether to make her speech now or when he had had his coffee. Perhaps he would feel more approachable when he'd had it. She decided to wait, carried in the coffee and offered the biscuits.

'Ah, rich tea,' murmured the professor. 'One of my favourite biscuits.' He made the observation blandly and she wasn't sure if he meant it or not, but presently decided that he had, for he ate all the biscuits on the plate.

She got more coffee and put out the rest of the biscuits and he ate most of those too. Megan's heart smote her. 'Would you like some sandwiches?'

'I had no time for lunch,' he told her, and managed to convey the impression of a starving man.

'I haven't had my supper. You're welcome to share it, that is unless you're on your way home. I expect your Mrs Thrumble will have a meal waiting.'

'I have to go back to Regent's before I go home.'

She got up. 'It's only cold ham and salad but I can make some toasted cheese.'

The nostrils of his splendid nose flared. 'Nothing could be tastier. Shall I make the salad or see to the cheese?'

She poked her head round the alcove. 'Can you cook?' she wanted to know.

'My mother was of the opinion that all boys should be able to fend for themselves. I boiled my first egg at a tender age—under supervision, of course.'

She swallowed a smile. 'If you'd really like to help, will you see to the toast and cheese, then?'

There was barely room for them both in the tiny kitchen and Meredith insisted on joining them so that every few minutes he had to be moved to a more convenient place but the professor, despite his great size, had an economy of movement, grating the cheese, making the toast, taking over the small cooking stove while Megan, rather squashed at the sink, made a salad. That done, she set the table, gave him two plates to warm and got out the ham. There wasn't much of it; she suspected that he could eat the lot with ease and then remembered with relief that she still had a cake in a tin. She had made it one evening, unable to settle with a book. She took it out; it looked all right and at any rate it would serve to fill him up if he was still hungry.

They sat down presently to a well made toasted cheese, a bottle of beer for him and a tonic for her, and, that polished off to the last crumb, they started on the ham and salad.

'You cook very well,' Megan said. 'What else can you do?'

'Make tea—an essential skill in this country—boil an egg, fry bacon.'

Megan had quite forgotten why he had come to see her. They started a trivial conversation which lasted through the coffee and several slices of cake.

'You are a splendid cook, Megan.' He sat back in his chair and Meredith promptly got on to his knee.

'Thank you, but if you're hungry I dare say food of any sort becomes delicious.'

She sat, her elbows on the table, her chin in her hands, feeling content. The professor was good company, he didn't need entertaining and when he spoke it was in a quiet voice which was most soothing. She was enjoying his company... She sat up suddenly. 'You came to see me about that orphanage. I said I would...'

'And the moment you put the phone down you had second thoughts. Very natural.'

She said waspishly, her feeling of content draining away, 'If you knew that, why did you bother to come?'

'Because you reacted as I expected you to and I think that by now, if you are quite honest with yourself, you may have seen the good sense in going away for a time.' When she remained silent he added, 'You have leave due to you and I think that things will be made as easy as possible for you given the—er—circumstances. Do you have a passport? Yes? Have you told Oscar of your in-

tention? I suggest that you do that and notice his reaction. If it is one of relief then you will know that you
have made a wise decision.'

He got to his feet. 'I must get back to Regent's. You
will be going home at the weekend? I will drive you down
and fetch you on Sunday evening.' He smiled suddenly.
'Don't worry, my dear, things have a way of sorting
themselves out without any help from us. Thank you
for my supper. We must do it again some time.'

She still hadn't spoken for the simple reason that he
hadn't given her the chance, and now she said, 'I shall
drive myself down at the weekend, but thank you for
your offer.'

They were at the door. 'I'll be here at half-past eight
on Saturday morning, and remember that you are going
to tell Oscar.'

'I—I haven't decided . . .' she began. She didn't finish
because he kissed her as he went out of the door. She
stood watching him talking to the boys, handing out
small change before he drove away with a casual wave.

'I have never met a man who annoyed me so much,'
she told Meredith, 'but there is no denying the fact that
he kisses very nicely.' She added fiercely, 'But I won't
be bamboozled.'

All the same, when she met Oscar on her way back
from her dinner the next day she told him about the
orphanage.

His eagerness for her to take the job was quite dis-
concerting. 'Just what you need to buck you up,' he said
enthusiastically. 'You don't want to get into a rut . . .' He
paused, 'You know I'm very fond of you, Megan; just
because we've broken up definitely doesn't mean that I
don't still care about you in a brotherly way. Who

hurt you to stay here for a week or two while you are deciding just where you want to go.' Her mother's voice was soothing. 'Do you want to talk to Melanie about it? She's over at the Howells's—Susan Howell is to be one of the bridesmaids.'

Megan said in a quiet little voice, 'Of course—no, she's been upset enough, hasn't she? If I just make all the arrangements and let her know when it's all settled.' She gave a small sigh. 'I told Oscar—he...thought it was a splendid idea.' She looked across at her father. 'So you think that I should go?'

'Tell me, Meg, why did you change your mind after you had agreed to go to Holland?'

'Well, I think I was annoyed because Professor van Belfeld took it for granted that I'd say yes...'

Her father smiled. 'A perfectly natural reaction which perhaps you have regretted since?'

She nodded. 'When he comes tomorrow I'll tell him that I will go...'

'When will that be, Meg?' her mother wanted to know. 'What about clothes?'

Clothes could, on occasion, be as efficient a panacea as a cup of tea.

'It's by the sea, this orphanage, quite a small place near a little town called Castricum, so I shouldn't want many clothes.'

'I do wonder if you wear uniform? You say the professor is on the board of directors; he might know. Does he go there often?' Mrs Rodner's voice was guileless.

'I shouldn't think he'd have time for that. I mean you can be on a board of directors and only meet now and again, can't you? He did say that he has consultant's work but I don't know where. He might even have a private practice—quite a few people pay for various tests, you know.'

'Well, now, your clothes,' urged her mother comfortably, and the rest of the evening passed agreeably in the choosing and discarding of the contents of Megan's wardrobe.

The professor arrived punctually on Sunday evening, accepted a cup of coffee from Mrs Rodner and sat for half an hour placidly answering all the questions she put to him, something made possible by Megan's absence. Half an hour before she expected him Melanie had phoned to ask if she could be fetched back home as the Howells's car had refused to start, and since Megan hadn't seen her during the weekend she had driven her father's car the few miles to the Howells's house, sure that she would be back home before he arrived. She had reckoned without the Howells, however, old friends who kept her talking for ten minutes or so before she and Melanie left them.

As they went into the house Megan said vexedly, 'He's here already...' and shot into the drawing-room with Melanie at her heels.

He got up as they went in, bade them a cheerful good evening and began to talk to Melanie. The orphanage wasn't mentioned and Megan gave a silent sigh of relief. Perhaps there hadn't been time for her mother to ask questions, and she was further reassured by the lady's observation that the professor had given her two special remedies against greenfly.

Megan drank her coffee, happily unaware of her mother's conversation with the professor, and presently assured him that she was quite ready to go if he wished. She fetched Meredith and stuffed him gently into his basket, bade them all goodbye, and stood quietly while he shook hands with everyone, saying something to Melanie which made her laugh before going with her to the car.

He started a conversation almost at once, rambling from one subject to another and giving her little chance to say much. She waited for him to bring up the subject of the orphanage but it wasn't mentioned, it was only as they were almost at the flat that she said without preamble, 'I'll go—I'll go to your orphanage. Everyone seems to think it's a good idea.'

'And you, Megan? Do you think it is a good idea?'

'Yes. I'm sorry I was difficult about it. I—I didn't mean to be. You've been very kind to go to so much trouble.'

'I would have done the same for anyone,' he assured her gravely.

At the flat he got out as he always did, unlocked her door, turned on the lights and inspected the kitchen door and window, but he didn't stay. As he went, he said, 'Allow me to see your matron before you arrange an appointment with her, Megan,' and when she looked surprised, he added, 'There will be no need for you to give reasons for leaving. She is, of course, aware that you have broken off your engagement to young Fielding but there will be no necessity to mention that.' He opened the door. 'I do not wish you to be hurt any more; you have had enough.' He laid a hand on her shoulder. 'I will see you some time during the week.'

For some reason, when he had gone, she burst into tears.

She had no need to make an appointment to see Matron; she was sent for the following afternoon. The ward was quiet and both part-time staff nurses were on duty. She straightened her cap, put on her cuffs and smoothed her dark blue uniform—Regent's was one of the hospitals which retained what were considered out-of-date uniforms for the nursing staff—and hurried down to the office. Her interview was surprisingly brief and Matron, a peppery autocrat of the old school, unbent sufficiently to wish her well.

'There is nothing like a change,' she observed in a surprisingly friendly voice. 'To widen one's field of work is always commendable, and when you return, Sister, if you care to get in touch with me, I dare say I can recommend you to several hospitals not in London. You have always given satisfactory work here and you can rest assured that you will receive the highest recommendations from myself and the medical staff.' She offered a hand which Megan shook. She hadn't uttered a word, for beyond a polite good-afternoon there had been no need, but now she spoke her thanks and said goodbye and got herself out of the office. She was to leave in a week's time; apparently the professor had arranged that, although Matron hadn't said so. She went back to the ward and found a message on her desk. She was to ring Professor van Belfeld as soon as possible.

His brisk, 'Van Belfeld, yes?' sounded businesslike.

'It's me,' said Megan, 'you left a message.'

'I shall come and see you this evening—about seven o'clock. No need to get supper; I'll bring some food with me. We can eat while we talk.'

She just had time to say, 'Very well,' before he rang off.

Jenny relieved her at five o'clock but she didn't leave the ward at once. She had the off-duty book to fill in, check the operation cases for the next day and go through the charts, so that it was almost six o'clock by the time she left the hospital, and since the professor had been vague about the time he intended to come she made haste to feed Meredith, put a tray ready for coffee and lay the table before doing her face and hair. She had thought about changing her dress—she was wearing a cotton crêpon dress, a shirtwaister in a honey colour—but she was convinced that the professor never noticed what she wore, and he could arrive at any moment.

'Really, this is becoming a habit,' she observed to Meredith, sitting in the easy-chair and washing his whiskers, 'and am I supposed to cook this supper he is bringing?'

Meredith paused long enough to gaze at her thoughtfully and then resumed his washing, taking no notice when a minute or two later the knocker was thumped.

Professor van Belfeld came in. His, 'Hello,' was cheerful as he put a plastic bag down on the table. 'Leave the door, will you?' he asked her. 'I'll fetch the rest.'

He came back with a cardboard box and put it beside the bag, closed the door with his foot and carried the box through to the kitchen.

'With an eye to the neighbours, I put the bottles in that bag. Could they go in the fridge?' He straightened up, taking up a great deal of room, and took the lid off the box.

'All cold,' he observed. 'I asked Mrs Thrumble to pack up an easy meal.'

Megan stood in the doorway since there was barely room for them both in the kitchen. 'How kind,' she said, not quite sure who was being kind, he for ordering the food or his housekeeper for packing it up. 'If you'd like to sit down I'll unpack it.'

He reached past her and put the wine in the fridge and went and sat down with the cat on his knee as she took the lid off the box.

'Heavens this is a cornu...' She tried again. 'A corn...'

'Cornucopia, the horn of plenty. Good, I told Mrs Thrumble that we were sure to be hungry.'

There was cold vichyssoise soup in a container, a raised pork pie, jellied chicken, hard-boiled eggs, potato salad, straw potatoes and a salad of tomatoes and apples with a garlic and walnut dressing, each in covered containers, and wrapped in a white napkin an apple pie with a pot of cream beside it. There were little crusty rolls too and a small crock of butter. Megan unpacked everything and laid the food out on plates and dishes.

'When do you want to have supper?' she asked, her mouth watering.

'As soon as it's on the table. Shall we have a drink first?'

He came into the kitchen and took a bottle from the fridge. 'It's probably not cold enough, though Thrumble chilled it well.'

'Champagne,' exclaimed Megan, 'that's for birthdays.'

'Celebrations, too.' He smiled at her. 'Fetch two glasses, there's a dear girl.'

She had no champagne glasses, only the all-purpose wine glasses she had brought from Woolworth's. 'Celebrations?'

'A new job, a new start in a new country—there's every reason to drink to that.' He eased out the cork, filled their glasses and handed her one.

Megan touched his glass and sipped. 'I don't know much about wines but this one tastes lovely.'

He agreed blandly; Bollinger 1985 was an excellent vintage champagne but he had no intention of telling her that. It was enough that she enjoyed it. He refilled their glasses and put them on the table and she fetched the soup.

It wasn't until they had started on the pie and chicken that he asked, 'Matron was helpful?'

'Yes, she couldn't have been kinder. She said that because of the circumstances I could leave in a week's time. What did you say to her?'

'Very little. I asked her if you might be released as soon as possible since it would be convenient for you to travel over to Holland with me.'

He poured some more champagne. 'Now, let us get the details clear, shall we?'

They finished their supper and Megan made coffee and took it to the table. As far as she could tell there was nothing left for her to do but pack a bag, find her passport and say goodbye to everyone. 'It is all so easy,' she observed. 'I thought leaving Regent's would be much more complicated.'

The professor agreed casually. He had spent time and thought and pulled a great number of strings to achieve the easiness.

He got up to go presently, packing the basket once more with the now empty containers, drying the coffee-cups as she washed them, and, that done, bidding her a quiet goodnight before driving himself home. The room seemed empty when he had gone, but, as she pointed out to Meredith, he was such a large man that he took up more space than anyone of a normal size.

She had wanted to ask him if she would see him once she got to Holland but he had a way of ignoring questions he had no wish to answer; he was too well mannered to offer a snub but it amounted to the same thing. She got ready for bed thinking about him. From an uncertain beginning they had become cautiously friendly, at least she had, and she found now that she didn't want to lose that friendship.

She wasn't on duty until ten o'clock the next morning, which gave her time to telephone her mother. 'That's settled,' said Mrs Rodner and Megan could hear relief in her mother's voice; it struck her then that if she went away for a time it might make things easier for Melanie and Oscar—perhaps they still felt guilty. 'The professor must be glad to be going home,' went on Mrs Rodner. 'However absorbing his work is here, he must miss his family.'

Megan agreed, and, after a few minutes gossiping, put down the phone. Until that moment she had come to regard the professor as someone who had a habit of turning up when most needed while at the same time remaining impersonally friendly, but now there was a danger of him becoming something more and her mother had reminded her of that. She was aware that she was interested in him and wanted to know more about him; what was more, she felt quite at ease with him, and that wouldn't do at all. She made up her mind to avoid him as much as possible and once she was in Holland she would thank him for his help and kindness and not see him again. The thought depressed her.

She told Jenny that she was leaving while they were snatching a cup of tea after their dinner-hour. Visitors were in the ward, and the operation cases were screened off in the side-cubicles with a student nurse checking them constantly and one of the part-time nurses keeping an eye on the other patients. Megan would go into the ward presently and walk round slowly so that anyone wanting to know anything could ask her; it was a system which worked very well for there was time to talk then whereas if relations waited until the ward closed before wanting to see her she was hard put to it to answer all their questions.

She got up now and went along to check on the operation cases, leaving Jenny to digest her news. All three of the ladies were sleeping. She took pulses, made sure that the drips were functioning correctly and inspected their dressings and then made her way round the ward, stopping whenever someone had a question to ask. It was twenty minutes or more before she got back to the office and Jenny had made a fresh pot of tea.

Megan sat down at her desk and Jenny asked, 'Who is taking over, Sister?'

'I've recommended you, Jenny. You've been here for two years now and you can run the ward as well as I can. Mrs Jeffs—one of the part-time staff nurses—has asked if she could do full-time; her son's going to boarding-school and her husband's been made redundant. You like her, don't you? And you get on well together. I've an appointment about it this afternoon but I've told you now so that if you don't want to take on the job you can warn me.'

Jenny wanted the job, although she said, 'Must you really leave, Sister? I know Regent's is a beastly neighbourhood but it doesn't take long to get to the shops and the theatres; won't you miss all that as well as the ward?'

'Well, I shall miss my friends and the ward, after all I've been here quite some time, but I do look forward to something quite different.'

'I wonder why Professor van Belfeld picked on you, Sister? He must know any number of nurses in Holland, he...' She stopped and went red. 'Oh, I'm sorry. I think I understand.'

'I want to get away from Oscar and my sister, Jenny, not because I mind them being engaged but because I think if I go away for a while they'll feel better about everything.' She spoke quietly. 'Besides, it is time I had a change.' She glanced at her watch. 'Time for the visitors to go; will you ring the bell, please? And I'll do another walk round.'

The busy days followed each other in the rigid pattern of hospital life and Megan saw nothing of the professor. He had told her to leave everything to him and she did. She went home on her day off, driving herself in her little car, and spending the day packing clothes to take to Holland. Spring was well on the way to summer and it bid fair to be warm weather; all the same she packed woollies and a long full jersey skirt and a handful of blouses.

'Someone told me that it rains a lot in Holland,' cautioned her mother, so she packed a rain jacket as well and a pair of sensible shoes. Melanie helped her to pack or at least sat on the bed and talked while Megan, a neat and tidy girl, folded dresses between layers of tissue paper.

'You'll be back for Christmas, won't you, Meg?' she asked.

'I should think so—probably in another job by then.' Megan surveyed a voile dress in pale green and peach. 'Do you suppose that I shall get a chance to wear this?'

'Why not? You're bound to make friends and go out with them. You will write and tell us about everything, won't you? Oscar says you're still apprehensive, but you're sure to meet lots of people. Do you suppose you'll see the professor often?'

'Probably not at all. I don't know where he lives in Holland; besides he'll have his wife and family.'

Melanie frowned. 'He still doesn't seem like a married man.'

Megan frowned too. Her heart had lurched at her sister's words and that really would not do. She didn't answer that but wondered out loud what would be the best way of getting Meredith home before she left. 'I think I'd better drive down on the evening before,' she said, 'and I can say goodbye then—we aren't going until an afternoon hovercraft.'

The last few days flashed by, her friends gave her a party in the nurses' home and she went back to the flat with an armful of presents and on the last day of all the nurses on her ward presented her with a little travelling clock. She went round the ward, wishing the patients goodbye and last of all said goodbye to Jenny, who wept a little. 'I shall miss you, Sister. I only hope I'll be as good at the job as you were and that you'll be very happy. Come and see us when you get back, won't you?'

'Dear Jenny, you'll be splendid in the job, and of course I'll look you up when I get back. I'll send you a card too...'

She was leaving the ward when the phone rang and she was asked to go to the path. lab. before she left the hospital.

She went at once, thinking gloomy thoughts about everything being cancelled at the last minute, the professor deciding not to go after all, and the orphanage not requiring her services. Her pretty face betrayed her doubts as she knocked at his office door and went in.

He was sitting at his desk writing, but he got up as she went in.

'Forgive me for getting you all the way up here but there are some reports which have to be finished this evening and I'm very pressed for time. I'll drive you and Meredith down tomorrow before we leave. Can you be ready at eight o'clock? You're sure you would rather take him to your home?'

'Yes, but there's no need——' began Megan.

'Be good enough not to waste my time, Megan.' He sounded testy. 'Just do as I ask. Perhaps your mother would be so kind as to give us coffee and sandwiches and then we shall have no need to stop on the way.'

'Very well, sir. I'll be ready in the morning. I'm sure Mother will be delighted to give us something.' She opened the door very quietly. 'Goodnight, sir.'

He had turned back to his desk. 'Goodnight, Megan.'

There was no reason why he should be friendly, she told herself as she went back to the flat; he had given her a much needed helping hand and seen her safely into a new job but there was no need to do more than that. She got supper, phoned her mother to explain that she wouldn't be going home until the morning and it would be the professor who would be driving her, and opened a can of sardines for Meredith as a special treat. She was going to miss him, but he would be happy at her home and when she was back in England and settled in another job and hopefully living out she would have him back.

She had packed up her small possessions already, seen the landlord and paid up her rent; it remained only for her to leave the key with the neighbours next door before she left in the morning. She set her alarm clock for six o'clock and went to bed, and Meredith, as usual, and probably under the impression that she didn't know he was there, crept close to her. She slept quickly, lulled by his contented purr.

CHAPTER SEVEN

MEGAN was ready, wearing the little grey jacket and the patterned skirt, her case and overnight bag and Meredith in his basket beside her, when the Rolls-Royce came to a quiet halt before the open door. The professor got out, wished her good morning and stowed the luggage while she took the key next door, lifted the cat basket on to the back seat and opened the door for her to get in. He did everything without apparent haste but all the same they were away in less than five minutes.

The professor drove in silence, only broken by Meredith's grumbling voice from the back of the car.

'I hope Meredith is going to be happy,' said Megan. 'He's always enjoyed being at home.'

'If he isn't and can't settle down, I'll bring him back to Mrs Thrumble.'

'You're coming back here?' She felt a pang of dismay. 'I thought you were going to stay in Holland.'

'I divide my time between here and there,' he told her blandly. 'I shall be in Holland for a time, examining and lecturing.'

It was still early enough for the traffic to be fairly light and he was driving steadily without much hindrance. 'We don't need to come this way to get to Dover, do we?' asked Megan.

'No. We can get on to the M25 and then the motorway to Dover. No problem.'

He began to talk about nothing in particular so that her last-minute doubts were soothed and the jumble of a hundred and one questions she had meant to ask were never uttered.

The whole family were there when they reached her home; Colin had been given leave to spend the day and her father hadn't gone to his office; they all came to the door as the professor stopped the car before it and bore them indoors, all talking at once. There wasn't a great deal of time; they had coffee, sitting round the kitchen table, eating the sandwiches Mrs Rodner and Melanie had made while Megan gave careful instructions about Meredith, who, to her relief, had got out of his basket and settled down with the air of a permanent resident beside a contented Janus. 'If he can't settle here, Professor van Belfeld says he'll have him; his house-keeper likes cats.'

The professor was at the other end of the table talking to her father, sitting casually as though he had all day in which to do nothing. Presently he caught her eye. 'If we leave in fifteen minutes?' he suggested.

He turned to Mr Rodner. 'Perhaps you would take a look at the engine? There are several things about it...'

The two of them went outside and Colin went with them and Melanie said softly, 'He's quite something, your professor, Meg. Well, all right, he's not yours, all the same, he is a dear—and that gorgeous car. Aren't you excited?'

'Yes, I think I am. It will be fun to try my hand at something different and I'll have time to decide what I want to do next.' Megan spoke brightly—a little too brightly, her mother thought.

'Is the professor staying in Holland?' she asked.

'I think so. He has some work to do there but I don't know where. I don't expect I shall see him again.' Megan sounded matter-of-fact. 'He's been very kind and helpful.'

Her mother agreed quietly. 'Indeed he has.' Quite unnecessarily so, she thought. It must have required quite an amount of thought and effort to have arranged for Megan to go to this job. After all, she could just as easily have found another post somewhere in England. She didn't believe that he was married and if he had led Megan to suppose that it was for his own good reasons. She felt in her bones that he was in love with Meg but Meg had given no sign of having any interest in him. She said now, 'Well, love, you had better get ready to leave. Telephone when you can and write long letters if you have the time. We'll take good care of your cat. Take care, Meg, and be happy.'

Saying goodbye was difficult; they weren't a very demonstrative family but they were close. Megan hugged everyone, including Janus and Meredith, and got into the car. It was foolish to feel childishly close to tears; she was a grown woman and past such things. She waved to the bunch of people on the doorstep, suddenly cheered by the professor's, 'We'll be back...' He didn't really mean that, of course, but it was nice of him to say something comforting.

They had upwards of a hundred and thirty miles to cover to Dover, for the most part on the motorways, and although he drove fast the professor had the air of a man with time on his hands, embarking almost at once on an undemanding conversation which continued on and off until they reached Dover. He had timed the journey well, for they went on board almost at once and over tea and biscuits Megan was able to study the guidebook of Holland he had thoughtfully provided for her. She had already looked up the area she was going to; the guidebook was more detailed, though, pointing out places of interest and commenting on even the smallest of villages. It seemed from the description that the orphanage was situated in the smallest of all—a handful of houses, a church and a shop which acted as a post office—but it was tucked away in the dunes, a short distance from the beach and nicely screened by a small wood. Castricum was no distance away and there were bound to be buses. The professor, deep in the papers he had taken from his dispatch case, looked up and smiled and she asked, 'Are there buses to Castricum and Heemskerk?'

'Certainly there are, although they dwindle during the winter. Everyone cycles; can you ride a bike?' She nodded. 'Good, there is bound to be one to spare for you. It's by far the best way to get around.'

He went back to his reading and she sat looking out of the window at the smooth water, conjuring up pictures of the weeks ahead of her.

The longest part of the journey was ahead of them; they drove from Calais to Gwent and Antwerp, crossed over into Holland and took the motorway to Rotterdam and then on to Hemestede and Leiden. The professor travelled fast and since the motorways circumvented the towns en route Megan had the merest glimpses of villages and churches. It was early evening now and she wondered how late it would be before they reached the orphanage. She hoped that there would be a meal and began to think of things she would like to eat, something which made her even more hungry. She looked guilty when the professor said, 'You must be hungry. It won't be long now.'

Presently he turned off the motorway into a narrow bricked road leading to pleasantly wooded country already dim in the twilight. The sea must be close now, thought Megan, but first, according to the guidebooks, there would be dunes. She had neglected to look at the signboards as they had turned off but a glimpse of water ahead of them reassured her, although there were no dunes, only small woods and open fields. The professor slowed as they approached a village and she looked around her—there was the church, a village square with the road running through it and houses clustered round it. There were two shops, she noted, and still no dunes, although the light was bad now and the car lights made the road ahead even darker. Through the village the professor turned the car into an open gateway, swept up a circular drive and stopped before the house.

'What a marvellous place for an orphanage,' declared Megan, being helped out of the car, her head swivelling in all directions in order to see everything at once. The house was indeed splendid, with white walls, heavy green shutters at its many large windows and a formidable door reached by double steps with wrought-iron railings.

The professor smiled faintly. 'This isn't the orphanage, Megan, it's my home.' Then at her thoughtful look, 'No, no, don't look at me like that. It is too late to take you to the orphanage this evening; you'll have a meal and spend the night here.'

He took her by the elbow and marched her towards the house but after a few steps she came to a halt. 'It really will not do, Professor van Belfeld. Does your wife expect me? Besides, you will want to be alone with her and your children.'

He took her by the shoulders and gave her a little shake so that the elderly man, thin and stooping, his hand on the door ready to open it, stared and decided to leave it closed for the moment.

'Let us get one thing clear. I have no wife, Megan, nor do I have any children.'

'But I said—you said...'

'Hush, and let me finish. I have never said that I had a wife and children. If you chose to think of me as a husband and father that was your concern and the result of a too vivid imagination...'

'Well, there was no need to be so secretive,' said Megan crossly. She caught his eye and added, 'Not that I am in the least interested in your private life.' She blushed as she said it. 'If you haven't a wife, however, I can't stay here.'

He had taken her arm and was walking her nearer the steps. 'My dear girl, only consider—am I, a member of the medical profession, likely to jeopardise my reputation? Come, come, I have always considered you a sensible young woman. I have a strait-laced grandmother staying, a married housekeeper of middle years, and two housemaids, both past their prime. Now will you come indoors? I'm hungry.'

There was no point in arguing further, indeed she suddenly wanted to laugh. She mounted the steps beside him, and the elderly man, timing the action nicely, opened the door as they reached it. His wrinkled face creased into a smile as they went in and he and the professor exchanged some words in their own language before the professor introduced him as Litman.

Megan shook hands and he said, 'You are most welcome, miss,' in heavily accented English. He said something to the professor, who laid a friendly hand on her shoulder.

'Stookje, one of the maids, will show you where you can tidy yourself before we see my grandmother. No hurry. I'll be here, waiting.'

She was led away to a cloakroom at the back of the hall, where she examined her face rather anxiously, feeling nervous about meeting the old lady, but she couldn't delay for too long; she tidied her hair and powdered her nose and went back into the hall to find the professor waiting for her.

The room they entered was beautiful with a high, elaborately plastered ceiling, the pale apricot walls echoing the colour of the heavy silk curtains at the long windows. A great fireplace dominated the room, flanked by bow-fronted display cabinets each filled with Delft Blue china. The floor was polished wood almost covered by thin old silk carpets and the chairs and two sofas were large and comfortable. A grand room, but lived-in.

There was someone in it now; an old lady sitting tall and erect and very straight in her chair. She had a quantity of white hair piled high above a thin, beaky-nosed face and was dressed in a pale grey dress of some fine material which owed nothing to modern fashion and formed a suitable background for the fine diamonds sparkling in the rings on her fingers. There was a ginger cat on her lap, who opened an eye as they went in and then closed it again, but the two dogs sitting by the old lady came across the room barking loudly and waving their tails—a golden Labrador and her companion, an elderly greyhound. They greeted the professor with delight and sniffed delicately at Megan's closed fist. 'Rosie and Swift,' murmured the professor, and urged her towards the old lady's chair.

He bent to kiss her elderly cheek, murmuring something which made her chuckle before introducing Megan. His grandmother held out her hand. 'I am delighted to meet you, my dear, even if only so briefly.' Her English was as faultless as her grandson's, betraying only the faintest accent. 'Perhaps we shall have time for a little talk before you go but now I am sure that you need your supper. I shall go to my room now but if you are not too tired will you come and see me before you go to bed? Just for a few minutes?'

Megan shook the bony hand gently. 'I should like that, Mevrouw van Belfeld; thank you.'

The professor had been standing and watching her. Now he said, 'We'll have a meal now, Grandmother, and I'll see that Megan visits you in about an hour.'

They had their supper in a small panelled room at the back of the hall, facing each other across a round table covered with white damask and sparkling with glass and silver and delicate china. For all the world, reflected Megan, tucking into asparagus soup, as though it were eight o'clock in the evening instead of almost midnight. The soup was followed by a smoked salmon soufflé and a salad, very good crème fraiche and early strawberries and coffee. Hardly a meal to induce early sleep but they had both of them had a long day and as far as she was concerned nothing would keep her awake once her head was on the pillow.

Litman had served them and they had talked little, and when they had finished their coffee the professor lost no time in accompanying her up the staircase to the gallery above. A number of passages led from it and he ushered her along one of them, tapped on a door at its end and urged her inside. The room was large, its wide windows overlooking a wide lawn and a circle of trees easily seen in the moonlight. It was furnished with heavy pieces in the Beidermeyer style and his grandmother was sitting in the middle of a vast bed, propped up by pillows, the ginger cat stretched out beside her, and she was reading but she put down her book as they went in and called, 'Come over here, child,' and patted the bed beside her. 'I shall not keep you long, and you, Jake, can go to bed. Mies shall take Megan to her room.'

The professor gave a grunt of amusement. 'You can see, Megan, how sternly my grandmother upholds the proprieties? I'll say goodnight.' He went over to the bed and kissed the old lady and then, much to Megan's surprise, kissed her too. 'Don't be late for breakfast,' he cautioned her. 'We have to make an early start.'

When he had gone, the old lady said, 'Sit on the bed, Megan—I'm a little deaf. Jake tells me that you have been working at the same hospital as he. A ward sister, were you not? And such a very pretty girl—surely you must be engaged to be married?'

Megan said, 'Yes,' and then, 'No,' and then, at her companion's request, told her a little about her home and family. Presently the old lady nodded in a satisfied manner. 'Jake has made a very good choice,' she observed. 'You will be very happy in Holland, my dear.' She turned a smiling face to Megan. 'You may kiss me goodnight, child. You will be gone long before I leave my room in the morning. It has been delightful meeting you. Mies will take you to your bedroom now.'

Megan bent to kiss the soft old cheek and was led away by a severe-looking Mies who, none the less, turned down the bed and drew the curtains in a pretty little bedroom on the other side of the gallery, then turned on the taps in the adjoining bathroom and wished her, '*Wel te rusten*.' Megan had no idea what she meant but it sounded kind.

A lovely house, she thought sleepily, curled up in her bed at last. What a pity I shall never see more of it.

There wouldn't have been time anyway; she and the professor breakfasted with a friendly speed and were on their way before eight o'clock. She had no idea in which direction he was driving now but presently she saw the dunes ahead of her and asked, 'Are we nearly there?'

'Yes—through this village.' They were passing through a cluster of houses around a church. 'And along this brick road. The sea is on the other side of the dunes.'

The orphanage was a long white building with a red roof, surrounded by a wide expanse of grass and ringed about by trees. Opposite the building at the far end of the grass was a flowerbed alive with colour and the professor broke the silence to say, 'The children all own a small plot of their own at the back of the orphanage to grow what they want.'

He drew up before a wide door, helped her out, clanged the great bell hanging on the wall and went inside to be met in the square hall by a motherly-looking woman with bright blue eyes and a cheerful face. She was stout and wearing a plain dark grey dress with a white collar and cuffs and a large watch pinned to her formidable bosom. She shook the professor's hand, greeting him like an old friend, and exchanged a few words with him before he introduced Megan. 'Megan Rodner, Katje—Megan, this is the directrice, Juffrouw Bal. She will talk to you presently but just now someone will show you to your room while we have a quick talk before I go. I must be in den Haag by half-past ten.'

Somehow she hadn't expected that. His home was such a short distance away and she had expected to see him several times before he went back to England. He was going to be in Holland for several weeks; he had told her that. Now she had a sudden panicky feeling that she would be left alone with no chance of seeing him again. But perhaps he would come back and see her...

His next words dispelled her hopes. 'I am sure you will be very happy here,' he told her, 'and return to England full of plans for the future.'

She stared up at him, her eyes mirroring her thoughts so clearly that his own eyes gleamed beneath their lids, but he said nothing more and shook her hand and wished her goodbye in his calm, friendly way. There was nothing more to do then but accompany the girl who had been summoned to show her to her room. Halfway up the stairs she turned to look at him. He wasn't even looking her way. She watched his vast person as he accompanied the directrice out of the hall, fighting down a strong wish to rush after him and tell him that she had no plans for the future, not if the future meant never seeing him again. It was a bit late in the day, she reflected sadly, resuming her climb, to discover that she was in love with him.

Her room was at the front of the house. It was small and sparsely but quite prettily furnished and it was spotlessly clean with rose-patterned curtains and bedspread. She went to look out of the window and the girl went with her. She had been introduced as Sine, a tall bony girl, a little older than Megan, but she had a nice open face and she was very friendly and spoke quite good English.

'A fine car,' she said as they stood looking down on the Rolls-Royce below. 'Professor Baron van Belfeld is a rich man. He is also most good and kind——'

'Baron?' asked Megan.

'You do not know that he is this?' Sine looked surprised. 'Perhaps in England he is Professor only?'

Megan nodded. Somehow knowing that he was a baron made him even more remote, although, she reflected sadly, as far as she was concerned now he could be a belted earl—if there were such a person in Holland.

Presently he and the directrice came out together, shook hands, and he got into his car and drove away. He hadn't looked up, but then why should he?

'That's that,' said Megan softly and then, 'I shall unpack? And is this the overall I am to wear?'

Sine nodded. 'You will please wear it and when you have unpacked you will go to the directrice. In fifteen minutes perhaps?'

'Very well, and thank you, Sine.'

Left alone, she unpacked quickly and tidied everything neatly away and got into the overall. It was pale blue cotton, nicely made and very well-fitting with short sleeves and a high collar. Beside it was a pile of white aprons and she hesitated about putting one on and decided against it. Sine hadn't been wearing one. She did her hair again, powdered her nose rather carelessly and went downstairs. She could hear the children now and babies crying, although there was no sign of anyone. She knocked on one of the doors in the hall with 'Directrice' painted on it and went inside.

The directrice was sitting at her desk and smiled at her as she went in.

'Do sit down, Miss Rodner. It must all seem strange to you but very soon you will feel comfortable. Sine will be with you and will show you round presently and you will meet the rest of the staff. Now I will tell you your duties. I wish you to work with the babies. We have seven at present; the youngest is not quite three months old, the oldest just one year. There is another girl who works with you alternately so that you have duty from three o'clock in the afternoon until ten o'clock at night when there is a girl for the night. In the second week your duty will be from seven o'clock each morning until three o'clock. You will have one day free each week when there is a part-time girl to relieve you. Sine will explain that to you. You relieve each other for meals and there are two extra girls on duty who can take over wherever they are needed. It is very hard work but most rewarding and you have time each day to yourself. You are a trained nurse? We have a small sickroom and if there should be illness I hope that you will undertake any nursing duties. You understand that the children are healthy; the older ones go to school in the village each day, and the little ones have a *kleurterschool* in the mornings. The babies have their own nursery but they are taken out of doors as often as possible.' She paused. 'I must tell you much, must I not? You are not alarmed?'

Megan smiled. 'Not at all, Directrice. It is a delightful change from London.'

'That is good. I myself have been in London in my youth. It is a fine city but I missed the sea and the country. Now Sine shall take you to drink coffee and then you will inspect everything. You will go on duty at three o'clock today and one of the part-time girls will be with you to show you all. I must tell you that my staff are called by their birth names; that is nicer for the children and for you all. What is your name, Miss Rodner?'

'Megan.'

The directrice nodded. 'A nice name.' She had touched the bell on her desk. 'Here is Sine.' She nodded dismissal. 'I hope you will be happy with us, Megan.'

The orphanage had been well planned. The rooms were light and decorated in pale colours; dormitories of eight or nine beds, a big playroom, a smaller room for the older children, and, running the length of the building facing the dunes, the nurseries, opening from each other with changing-rooms for the babies and cots widely spaced. A balcony ran their whole length, covered in and with sliding glass panels to shut out the wild winter weather; Sine assured Megan that it was common enough. Last of all she was taken to the sickroom, well equipped with two cubicles with a bed in each and another screened off with a cot. There was everything here needed if there should be an emergency. Megan remarked upon it and Sine said, 'We are not near a big hospital, so it is necessary that we are prepared.'

'Is there a doctor who comes?'

'Yes. Each week he visits and also in time of need.' She led the way downstairs. 'We will drink coffee and then you will go and look outside.'

They had their coffee in a small room furnished with square tables seating four and here again the walls were painted in a pretty shade of blue and the curtains were a darker blue of some thick material and drawn well back from the windows. There were several older girls in the room and Megan was introduced to them each in turn, confused by their various names but relieved to find that they all spoke English of a sort. Even if she was to be there for a short time she would do her best to learn some Dutch at least. She had had the foresight to bring a dictionary with her; she could study it when she was free.

The girls were kind and very friendly. 'Tomorrow,' said Sine, 'you will be free in the morning and one of us will go with you to the village so that you may then go alone.'

'Letters? The post office?' asked Megan.

'There is a *postkantoor* in the village and also the *postbode* comes each day; you may give him letters. Also there is the *telefoon* in the hall, and we may use it. I show you.'

All the basic needs, thought Megan, and, coffee finished, went to her room to get notepaper and envelopes and small change. She phoned her mother first, ringed round by willing helpers, and then, a cardigan over her overall since the wind from the sea was chilly, she found her way into the grounds around the orphanage. There was a revolving chalet beyond the sweep of grass and behind the building rows of small garden plots—the children's—and beyond those a well kept kitchen garden. There was a gate in the fence which separated the grounds from the dunes and a path beyond leading to a short flight of wooden steps which presumably led to the sands beyond. She would have liked to have explored further but she had been warned that the midday meal was served in two shifts and she was to go to the first one at twelve o'clock. There was just time to write a quick note home, and, if she had the leisure still, a polite note to the professor, thanking him for his help. The writing of it hung over her head like a cloud but it was something that would have to be done. She would have to ask the directrice where to send it for she hadn't asked the name of his house or what the village was called and he hadn't volunteered any information. Perhaps he didn't want her to know. She resolutely dismissed him from her mind and embarked on a cheerful letter home. She had it finished with five minutes to spare before her dinner and went indoors to join whoever was in the dining-room.

Sine was there, waiting for her and the two other girls at the table were introduced: Helene and Anneke. Anneke was to work with Megan in the nursery that afternoon, a stoutly built girl with a pretty round face and rosy cheeks.

She spoke basic English, but Helene beyond a few words didn't. Nevertheless, they all got on splendidly together eating *gehakt balletjes*, the Dutch version of rissoles, boiled potatoes and carrots. There was yoghurt to follow, and big cups of coffee. Plain fare but well cooked. 'This evening at six o'clock,' explained Sine, 'there is the *brood maaltijd*—the bread meal, again with coffee.'

She didn't explain further and Megan didn't like to ask; it sounded a bit frugal but looking around her at the healthy-looking girls at the tables she consoled herself with the thought that there would probably be something to put on the bread.

There were still a couple of hours before she needed to go on duty and when Anneke offered to show her the way down to the shore she decided to leave the letter to the professor and go with her. They went through the gate and along the path between the dunes and up the few wooden steps. The sea lay before them, coldly blue, and as far as they could see on either side of them there was a wide stretch of golden sand stretching into the distance.

'Nice?' asked Anneke.

'Lovely, I had no idea. Do the children come here?'

'The bigger ones, yes, but not the babies. When you are free you can walk for kilometres—up to den Helder or down to Haarlem.' She laughed. 'But not in the winter, for it is cold then.' She added, 'But then you will not be here.'

A pity, thought Megan; to walk along the sand in the teeth of a howling gale and with the sea crashing on to the beach would be an experience. Preferably with the professor... she crushed the thought—it was no good thinking about him. She told herself this every hour or so without any success.

Once in the nursery, however, she had little chance to think about him or anything else. The babies provided a constant round of feeding, changing, bathing, and in some cases—the three older ones—amusing. Anneke was a tower of strength and patience, making sure that she knew where everything was and giving her titbits of information about each baby. They were well-cared-for and there was time to cuddle them. 'Are they all orphans?' asked Megan.

'Yes—how do you say?—abandoned. Little Jan——' she nodded towards the smallest baby that Megan was feeding '—he was found in a paper bag in the dunes. He was then a few days old but he is now a handsome boy, is he not?'

Megan stared down at the scrap she was cuddling. 'He's beautiful. And he'll be happy here.'

'Lise, over there in the second cot—the professor found her in a street in Beverwijk. He has a great interest in the children.'

'I'm sure he is a very kind man,' said Megan, her cheeks pink.

She was left on her own after that first day. The directrice did a round of the orphanage twice a day, a leisurely walk, taking the time to talk to the staff and children alike, and, beyond asking Megan if she was quite happy, she had no comment. It was hard work but she enjoyed it and there was no time to sit around and be sorry for herself, and when she was off duty there was always someone else free to show her the village or the dunes or walk along the sands. At the end of the week she changed to the morning shift so that she was free each afternoon and when she had her first day off she borrowed a bike and took herself off to Castricum. It was a pleasant little town with a few shops and a restaurant in Dorpsstraat where she had some lunch before cycling on, going north to Egmond, where she parked the bike and had tea on the boulevard. She felt nicely filled with fresh air as she made her way slowly back to the orphanage. She was thinking about the professor, of course, wishing with all her heart that he were there with her. 'He will have forgotten me by now,' she mused sadly, 'but he was quite right persuading me to come here. I'm too busy to think about me and when I'm free it's so peaceful.'

She had written him a letter, of course, a stiff little note which had taken her hours to compose. The professor had read it and smiled a little and folded it carefully and put it in his waistcoat pocket. He would be in Holland for several weeks and he had every opportunity to go to the orphanage and see her, but, much though he wished to do so, he didn't; he was a man who could bide his time and Megan must have the time to listen to her own heart.

She made friends with the other girls well and quickly enough; within days she was trying out a few words of Dutch and they encouraged her, took her with them when they shared her free time, cycling or walking along the golden sands, or going to the village for stamps or to post their letters. She wrote letters; any number, for she had plenty of friends at Regent's as well as her family. She had sent a postcard to Oscar extolling the beauties of her surroundings and saying how much she liked her work. The only person she didn't write to was the professor; she had written that once, and sent it, on the directrice's advice, care of the hospital in Leiden. She hadn't expected to have a reply but she had hoped for one.

She was halfway through her second week and busy with the ten o'clock feeds for the babies when the directrice came into the nursery and with her a youngish man. He was of middle height and stockily built, with fair hair and a pleasant open face and dressed in trousers and a light jacket over an open-necked shirt.

'Dr Timuss,' said the directrice. 'He visits us regularly and will come in an emergency.' She smiled at Megan. 'And this is Megan, who has come from England for a little while Mien is in Canada.' She nodded at them both. 'Now I shall leave you to show Dr Timuss round the nursery, Megan, and do not be afraid; he speaks very good English.'

Dr Timuss grinned cheerfully. 'Have you had any chance to try your Dutch yet?'

Megan laughed. 'Almost none at all. Does everyone speak English in Holland?'

'No, no, not everyone, but most of us. And we are always delighted when we have an opportunity to air it.' He smiled. 'Now where shall we start? Have you any problems?'

'Well, no, I don't think so. Jantje isn't a very happy baby but perhaps that's because he was left in a paper bag; he feeds well and he loves to be cuddled. He's putting on weight.'

She had picked the baby up and tucked him under one arm. He looked bad-tempered but he didn't cry and when the doctor took him from her he gave a small grunt of satisfaction. 'Poor little devil,' said Dr Timuss, 'but once we've got him going he will be fine. How's our Lise doing? She was so ill when the professor brought her here. You've met him, of course?'

Megan was vexed to feel her cheeks grow warm. 'Yes, I was at Regent's in London. It was he who found this job for me.'

'He's a fine man. A bit crusty but quite brilliant.' He handed Jan back and they went on round the cots and as he left he said casually, 'I've a practice in Castricum; perhaps when you're free one day I might be allowed to show you something of the country round here.'

'Why, thank you, I should like that.'

'Good. We must fix a day soon.' He nodded goodbye and left the nursery and she went back to the feeds and the chores which made up her hours of duty. She forgot him at once for, however hard she tried, she was unable to prevent her thoughts turning to the professor. Crusty or not, there was no other man in the world for her.

CHAPTER EIGHT

THE following week on her day off Megan went to Alkmaar, cycling to Castricum and catching a bus for the less-than-ten-mile journey. Alkmaar, she had been told by her newfound friends, was well worth a visit, especially as her day off happened to be on a Friday when there was the famous cheese market. The bus took her through the town to the building where the cheeses would be sold and she joined the crowd of sightseers to watch the porters carrying the cheeses on a kind of wooden stretcher to a ring where the selling took place, and, when the sale had been completed by a clasping of hands, the cheeses were loaded on to the stretchers again and the porters, each with a leather strap around his neck attached to the stretcher, jogged away with their load. All the while the carillon played until noon when the doors of the bell tower opened and to the accompaniment of trumpeting figures horsemen circled the tower. Megan, enjoying every moment enormously, craned her neck to see with the rest of the tourists and then turned her steps towards the main street, intent on coffee and a *kaas broodje*. There were plenty of cafés to choose from, and she was standing undecided outside one of them when she was tapped on her shoulder and Dr Timuss wished her a cheerful goodday. 'Sight-seeing?' he wanted to know. 'If you have nothing better to do have some lunch with me—I had to come to the hospital here and I have no surgery until five o'clock.'

'Oh, how nice.' Megan beamed at him; she had enjoyed her morning and she had been contemplating an afternoon of sightseeing but all the same she had been feeling lonely. 'I was going in here...'

'Fine for a sandwich, but I'm hungry.' He took her arm and steered her through the crowds and turned in at De Nachtegaal Hotel, where he asked for a table by the window and sat down opposite to her. 'A sherry?' he suggested and when a waiter handed her a menu he asked, 'Will you let me choose for you? Smoked eel on buttered toast, a ham salad with *pommes frites* and one of our magnificent ice-creams to finish.'

He ordered and began an easy conversation; was she happy at the orphanage? Did she like what she had seen of Holland? Did she intend to see the country before she returned to England? 'You are only here for a few weeks, the directrice tells me—have you a job to go back to?'

She shook her head. 'No. I wanted a change. I think that I may stay in Holland for a little while; I'd like to see Amsterdam and Delft and perhaps the Hague.'

The eels came and she pronounced them delicious; so was the ham salad. He had offered her wine and when she refused he hadn't pressed her but ordered tonic for her and a Pils for himself. He was a good companion and she felt at ease with him, and when over the promised ice-cream he asked her if he might show her the St Laurenskerk she agreed happily. 'It will be closed,' he told her, 'but I can get the key from the custodian and he will show us round.'

The church was at the top of the town and they didn't hurry. There were shops to linger before and old buildings to be admired and when they finally reached the church there was a great deal to see in it. The tomb of Floris the Fifth who had fought the Frisians, for one thing, and the splendid organ. It was after three o'clock when they emerged into the street at last and Dr Timuss said, 'A cup of tea? I'll drive you back, unless you had planned to stay until the evening?'

'I was going to get back in time for the six o'clock meal,' she told him.

'Splendid, let's find a café. There's a nice little place along here.'

They had tea—hot water in tall glasses with a tea bag in the saucer—and enormous cream cakes, while Dr Timuss told her about his fiancée, Imogen, in her last year at Groningen University, studying medicine. 'We shall marry next year and have a partnership. Castricum is getting bigger from year to year and there is work enough for us both.'

'How very nice,' said Megan. 'Tell me about her—is she dark or fair...?'

It was like taking the cork out of a bottle. By the time they reached the orphanage she knew everything there was to know about Imogen. Rather belatedly he asked, 'And you, Megan—do you have the prospect of marriage?'

She told him quietly that no, she hadn't, and he was too polite to ask any more questions. She thanked him for his company and bade him a friendly goodbye. At the evening meal later she described her day to the girls sitting at her table. 'It was nice meeting Dr Timuss. I would never have seen the church if he hadn't known how we could get inside. I thought I would go to Haarlem one day; there's a splendid church there, isn't there?'

The meal ended with everyone making suggestions as to where she should go for her next free day. 'So much to see,' said Anneke, 'and you have but a few weeks.'

The days became warm and sunny, the cots were wheeled out on to the balcony each morning and the older babies crawled and staggered around their playpens. Megan was happier than she had been for weeks; she was busy—too busy to brood over her own unhappiness, for she had friends among the other girls and there was always something with which to fill her free hours. Best of all she liked to walk along the sand at the water's edge with one or other of the girls, listening to their gossip, learning a little Dutch and laughing at her own mistakes. True, the professor was never far from her thoughts, but life, she reminded herself, had to go on. In a few weeks she would go back to England and start again. A week or so at home while she made up her mind where she wanted to go and then the worrying search for a post as a ward sister. Oscar and Melanie had decided to settle in Kent or Sussex. Oscar had been offered a post as Senior Registrar at one of the London teaching hospitals and since Melanie firmly refused to live there they planned to buy a small house near enough for him to get home in his free time until such time as he could get a partnership in a general practice. It would be better, Megan had decided, to get right away from London for a time at least. She reflected that it would have been nice to have stayed on at the orphanage where there were no reminders of her unhappy past few months and where there was always the chance that she might see the professor again, but that was very unlikely.

She was to be proved wrong. Two days later she was standing at the end of the nursery with Dr Timuss; she had Jantje tucked under one arm and they had paused in his round so that he might show her a photo of his Imogen.

The professor, coming quietly into the nursery, paused in the doorway watching them, his face expressionless as she lifted a laughing face to her companion and then bent with him over the photo. He stood quietly for a few moments and then began to walk leisurely towards them. It was Dr Timuss who heard him first and went to meet him, hand outstretched. 'Professor...' They shook hands and he went on talking in Dutch. The professor answered civilly but his eyes were on Megan, who was clutching Jantje and blushing vividly. Her heart thumped so hard that she was afraid that it might disturb the baby and even if she had wanted to speak she had no breath to do so.

Presently the two men joined her and the professor said, 'Good morning, Megan. You are enjoying your work here?'

'Very much, sir.' Her cheeks weren't pink any more but pale. She looked at his handsome, calm face and could see only austere civility, so that the sudden warm glow she had felt at the sight of him turned slowly cold.

What had happened, she wondered, to change him from the friendly man he had become during those weeks in London to this coolly impersonal stranger? She wished that he hadn't come; to have remembered him as a friend was painful enough even when he had gone away without a proper goodbye but now he was looking at her as doubtless he had looked at the nurses at Regent's who were scared of him. Not that *she* was scared of him, she told herself. She stood quietly, still cuddling Jantje until he said with that same cool civility, 'Don't let me hinder you, Sister. I just want a chat with Dr Timuss.'

So she put Jantje back in his cot and wheeled it out on to the balcony and took Lise away to be changed and fed. When she came out of the changing-room the men were no longer there.

She couldn't leave the nursery otherwise she would have looked out of a window to watch if the professor had gone. 'And a lot of good that would be,' she told Lise as she wheeled her out on to the balcony beside the other babies. All the same, when she was relieved for her midday dinner she crossed the landing and peered out of the window. The Rolls-Royce was still there: if she hurried she might get a glimpse of him on her way to the dining-room. She was turning away when he came out of the door with Dr Timuss and the directrice and she craned her neck to see him better, only to withdraw it smartly when he suddenly looked up. His look held hers for a moment but he didn't smile; indeed, he could have been looking at a blank wall. She felt the tears in her eyes and dashed them away angrily. Why, oh, why, she thought wildly, must I love someone as tiresome as a stiff-necked professor who doesn't care a row of pins for anyone? By 'anyone' of course she meant 'me', but she wasn't going to admit that. She went on down to the dining-room. 'I hope I never see him again,' muttered Megan, knowing that she didn't mean a word of it.

The professor drove himself to his home where, under the eye of Litman, he made a pretence of eating his lunch and then whistled to the dogs and went for a long walk, and as he walked he bent his considerable mental powers to the problem of Megan. She had looked beautiful in the nursery that morning—she had also looked so happy laughing up at that whippersnapper Timuss. The professor ground his splendid teeth quite viciously at the memory, while at the same time conceding that she was young and so was Timuss whereas he was nearing his fortieth year... and he loved her and deep inside him he knew that she loved him although perhaps she didn't know that yet. He had to let her find that out for herself. It might take time but he was a man of patience. He tramped back to his home and ate the splendid dinner set before him by a gratified Litman; he had resolved to do nothing to attract Megan. He was aware that he could, if he wished, gain her love—he was aware too without conceit that he was attractive to women—but he didn't want that; he would do nothing to encourage her.

There was a mass of work waiting for him in his study, so he put all thought of Megan out of his head and sat down at his desk until after midnight. It was a great pity that he didn't know that she was lying in her bed crying her eyes out because she was quite sure that she would never see him again.

The annual picnic, one of the major events of the orphanage's year, was to be held during the following week. It was no mean affair of Thermos flasks and sandwiches; preparations started several days before the great day, and the orphans were in a high state of excitement, the older ones allowed to help. The weather was splendid, the days warm and sunny, and although Megan found the sea breeze a bit much no one else appeared to notice it. On the morning of the picnic there was a constant stream of people going along the path through the dunes and up the wooden steps laden with covered trays and buckets, folding chairs and massive sunshades, buckets and spades for the children, beach balls and towels. Megan, bathing the babies, wondered if she would have a chance to go. She was off duty at three o'clock that day but it seemed unfair to leave Sine, who was doing the alternate duty with her, alone with the little ones. She broached the subject at midday dinner, taken early on account of the picnic, and was told that all the babies would be going to the beach too. 'They will have had their feeds and the older ones will have their tea on the beach. We've got carrycots for the tinies.' The other girl beamed at Megan. 'I shall come on duty a little early and bring help so that we can all go together, you will see.'

Sure enough Sine, Anneke and several people Megan hadn't met before arrived well before three o'clock and the business of packing the three small babies into carry- cots and the older ones securely tucked under willing arms got under way. The older children had already gone down to the beach, pushing and shoving each other and screaming with delight, and now the nursery party began its careful journey. A gated staircase led from the balcony to the ground below and Megan, coming last with a peevish Jantje in his carrycot, bolted the gate behind her while Anneke, carrying Lise, waited for her.

'The babies must return for their feed and supper at six o'clock,' said Anneke. 'I will come back with Sine— they will be cross by then and difficult.'

'No, I'll come,' Megan told her. 'You're on duty at ten o'clock; it makes too long a duty for you and I've nothing to do this evening. I'd like to, really I would.'

The sand, when they reached it, was alive with children and the entire staff, although there was no sign of the directrice.

'She comes presently,' said Sine as they arranged the babies under the sunshades and settled the bigger ones on the sand to play. 'I think it is good that Anneke sits with the cots and we will play with the older ones.'

The two oldest babies, Thomas and Wilma, were very nearly a year old, barefoot, and, armed with buckets and spades, Megan took them down to the water's edge where the sand was firm and while Sine sprawled on the sands with Dirk and Nel, who were at the crawling stage, they played.

There was a lot of noise, but it was a nice noise of children being happy. Megan, kneeling on the damp sand, became absorbed in showing her small charges how to make sand pies. The sudden silence made her look up; coming down the wooden steps was the directrice, followed by several people. An elderly bearded man hard on her heels; an elegant lady, quite unsuitably dressed for the occasion; another younger lady, wearing what the fashion magazines would have described as casual wear of the most expensive kind, and behind her two men, Dr Timuss and the professor.

Some of the older children had joined Megan by now, anxious to add to the rather battered pies Thomas and Wilma were labouring over, so that she was well screened from all but the most searching gaze. Besides, she had prudently turned her back on the party now strolling amongst the children.

The professor had seen her at once although he made no move to seek her out, but presently the whole party, with the directrice leading, fetched up beside her and she had to scramble to her feet.

'This is our English helper, who is filling Mien's post while she is in Canada with her parents. She is a trained nurse and we are most fortunate to have her. Megan, these ladies and this gentleman are members of the board of directors of the orphanage. You know Professor van Belfeld, so I do not have to introduce you to him.'

Megan shook hands, smiled at Dr Timuss and said, 'How do you do, Professor?' her eyes on his tie, and was thankful that at that moment Thomas whacked Lise with his spade and created a diversion.

If she had hoped that everyone would go away she was mistaken. The directrice and the two ladies wandered off, following the bearded gentleman in earnest conversation with Dr Timuss, and that left the professor, who scooped Thomas tidily off the sand and said placidly, 'The actual picnic is about to begin; bring Wilma along before all the cakes and ice-creams are eaten.'

There was nothing to do but go with him, still carrying Thomas, grizzling into his shoulder. The professor didn't seem to mind the wet little face against his chin and the small damp sandy hands leaving patches on his suit. Megan, forgetting to be haughty, observed that the patches would leave seawater stains. 'You'll have to get that suit cleaned or it will be spoilt,' she pointed out.

They were halfway up the beach and he stopped to look at her. 'You sound like a good wife should sound but you look...' he paused '... you don't look like one.'

She said frostily, 'Well, I don't suppose I do.' She couldn't prevent her gaze from resting on the young lady in the casual outfit, sitting under an umbrella, sipping tea, looking cool and with not a crease to be seen on her pristine crispness. She looked away and caught the professor's eye upon her. 'Of course I don't!' she said snappily, aware that her hair was blowing all over the place and that her blue overall was no longer as clean as it might be. 'Thank you for carrying Thomas; we're going to have our tea with Sine and Dirk and Nel.'

The professor didn't seem to have heard her. He deposited a now cheerful baby boy on the sand and folded his enormous length beside him, giving him a biscuit to eat and helping himself to a sandwich before starting a cheerful conversation with Anneke, and when Sine came she joined in as well so that Megan found herself one

of a bunch of grown-ups and toddlers enjoying themselves on an early summer's day. Not for long, though;
the picnic would continue for an hour or two more but
the babies would have to go back to the nursery. Megan
glanced at her watch and then at Sine.

'Shall we take the babies first and then one of us can
come back for the others?' They got to their feet and
the professor got up too just as the younger lady saun-
tered across towards them.

'Jake...' she began coaxingly and Megan, all ears,
deplored the fact that the Dutch language was still a
mystery to her when it came to conversation.

He stood listening with a half-smile and then nodded
his head. They were planning an evening together, decided Megan, her imagination running riot. She hoisted
up the carrycot with Jantje, awake and bawling for his
feed, and started for the steps. Sine was behind her with
Lise and unexpectedly, the professor with the third
infant—Paul—a stolid four-month-old boy, still happily
asleep.

The nursery safely gained, she thanked him quietly,
wished him goodbye and set about tucking in babies in
their cots while Sine fetched their bottles. The professor
wasn't to be hurried, however; he asked gently, 'So
anxious to be rid of me, Megan?' Then, when she didn't
reply, he enquired, 'You find enough to do in your free
time? I dare say you have made friends. Have you seen
anything of Holland yet?'

She had Jantje on her lap while he bellowed. 'Oh, yes,
thank you, and I have made several friends, everyone is
so kind... and I've explored Castricum and Alkmaar. I
met Dr Timuss there and he kindly showed me the
church...'

'A sound young man,' said the professor, at his most urbane.

He went away presently to return with Anneke and the first of the older children and this time Dr Timuss was with him—he popped Wilma into her cot and came over to stand by her while she fed a now content Jantje.

'A splendid picnic, Megan. You enjoyed it? Are there any other babies who need to be looked at before we all go home?'

'No, they're all fine.' She smiled at him. 'It was a wonderful afternoon and the children simply loved it.'

'A pity you won't be here for Christmas. That is also an occasion, is it not, Professor?'

The professor agreed blandly and added, 'I must be going; I've promised to take Juffrouw ter Mappel to Leiden.'

'A charming lady. You do not return to England yet, Professor?'

'Not just yet. Give me a ring about the new equipment you need, will you? There's a directors' meeting next week and I'll see that you get it.'

The two of them went away, bidding a casual goodnight as they went.

'So that's that,' muttered Megan to a replete and drowsy Jantje.

The two men paused on the landing outside the nursery to watch the first of the older children begin their reluctant straggling back to the orphanage.

'Next year I'll have my wife to help me,' observed Dr Timuss. 'She will be a great help here with the children...'

The professor turned to look at him. 'You are to marry? I did not know. A recent engagement? Is your marriage to be soon?'

Dr Timuss, happily unaware of the truly ferocious look in his companion's eyes, went on, 'Next year—she will have to get used to life with a GP, but I'm sure she will settle down.' He added boyishly, 'I never thought, when we met, that she would have me.'

The professor was standing at the windowsill, his hands in his pockets, watching the children. 'I must congratulate you and your bride and wish you both very happy.'

'Thanks, Professor. Imogen will be coming to stay for a week very shortly—I do hope it will be before you go back to England...'

'Imogen?'

'A charming name, isn't it? She's a clever girl, too; she takes her finals in three months.'

'I shall be delighted to meet her.' Something in the professor's voice made Dr Timuss look at him but his calm features were, if possible, calmer than ever, and his voice betrayed nothing of his feelings as he observed, 'Well, I must go and find Juffrouw ter Mappel. Good night, Timuss. The picnic has been a success; it always is.'

He went on down the stairs and out into the grounds to meet Juffrouw ter Mappel as she crossed the grass. Megan, with Lise over one shoulder, bringing up her wind, stood at a window and watched them...

Off duty at last, she agreed with everyone else that it had been a marvellous day. 'Do the directors always come?' she wanted to know.

'Of course but they do nothing, only Professor van Belfeld joins us and the children—he is a good man, for he pays for most of it too.'

'The younger lady who came is very pretty,' observed Megan, hoping to hear more about her.

'Juffrouw ter Mappel?' asked Sine. 'She is a most handsome lady and very rich. She would I believe like to marry the professor but he does not look at her.'

With which grain of comfort Megan was forced to be content, although it didn't prevent her from having a nice quiet cry once she was in bed.

On her next day off she went to Leiden. It was a place of great interest; she had been told its buildings were old and full of history. There were museums, its magnificent Sint Pieterskerk, the university, the street where Rembrandt was born, picturesque almshouses, and, added Anneke, very practically, there were some fine shops if she wished to buy presents to take home.

All of these sufficient reason to visit the historic town, although of course the one reason which really mattered was the fact that the professor, according to odd pieces of gossip she had understood, was lecturing at the medical school there. Not that she wished to meet him, Megan told herself, but it would be nice to see where he was working. She took an early morning train from Castricum and got to Leiden in nice time to sit in a small café drinking her coffee and watching the busy Breestraat before her. She had collected a leaflet from the VVV Office outside the station and now she turned her attention to it, deciding where she would go. Obedient to its advice, she inspected the Lakenhal, then went back to the Breestraat, intent on visiting the town hall. She would, she decided, do her sightseeing before lunch and devote the afternoon to buying presents to take home. After the town hall were the famous almshouses where she lingered, soothed to a quiet content by ageless beauty before she wandered on to the church, vast and lofty and timeless. It was well after noon by the time she left and there was still the Rapenburg Canal and the university to see. She decided to have a meal first and, primed by advice from some of the friends in the orphanage, she went to the *pannekoekhuis* where she ate a very large pancake filled with crisp bacon and drank more coffee before starting off again.

She took the opposite side of the canal to the university and as she approached it, looked cautiously across the water, reassured to see that there wasn't a soul in sight. She was passing the Museum van Oudheden, a vast building which she mistakenly believed was sheltering her nicely just in case the professor should appear on the opposite side of the water, but there was still no sign of anyone and she lingered a moment; it was something she would want to remember, just as she wanted to remember everything to do with the professor.

Presently she turned and walked back the way she had come, not daring to cross to the other side, happily unaware that the professor, standing at one of the apparently blank windows, was watching her with great interest and pleasure because she was so obviously alone. He began to whistle as he made his way through the building, for he was examining students that afternoon. Even if he had been free to go after her, he wouldn't have done so; he was an angler of no mean repute and he knew the skills of playing his fish would pay off if he had patience. Megan wasn't to be hurried and she must be quite sure. That he himself was sure had nothing to do with the matter, and he had no intention of coercion.

Megan, with a last look at the Rapenburg Canal and its impressive buildings, took herself off to the shops, to buy Delft Blue china, silver coffee spoons, cigars and, after careful thought, an illustrated book of the historical towns of the Netherlands; a suitable gift for Oscar, she considered, being quite impersonal. Content with her purchases, she went to the Rotisserie Oudt Leyden, close to the station, and had a very expensive tea. There was only one large restaurant in Castricum where the food was good but certainly not four-star; she might not have the opportunity to have a meal as splendid as the one she was eating now. She would be leaving soon now although she didn't know exactly when and rather than go to Amsterdam or den Haag she had decided to see as many of the smaller towns as possible. The train service was good; she could go to Enkhuizen or Medemblik on the Ijsselmeer and spend a day—and perhaps also to Delft. That left Utrecht, Arnhem and Apeldoorn, all of which she had been urged to visit, but she doubted if she would have the chance to go to them.

By the time she got to Castricum it was too late for the evening meal at the orphanage, so she went to t'Eethuisje and had an *uitsmijter* and coffee before catching a bus back.

It was several days later, while she was bathing Jantje, that the directrice came into the nursery. She bade her good morning and waited while Megan wrapped the baby in a warm towel and set him on her lap.

'Don't stop your work, Megan. I come merely to tell you that in two weeks you may return to England. The exact day I cannot yet tell but I am sure you will wish to know so that you can tell your family and perhaps make preparations to obtain work when you return.'

Megan dried a peevish Jantje, sprinkled him with talcum powder and clothed him in a nappy and a zipper suit. 'Thank you, Directrice,' she said quietly, 'that gives me plenty of time to make my plans. I shall be sorry to leave here.' She brushed the pale feathers of Jantje's hair into neatness and dropped a kiss on the back of his neck. 'I shall miss the babies.'

'We shall, all of us, miss you, Megan. If there had been a vacancy on the staff I would very much have liked you to stay.' She glanced at Megan, 'You are well, my dear? You are pale—you do not work too hard?'

'Oh, no, Directrice—and I feel very well...'

'I shall go now, for you have your morning's work. If you wish to know anything, or I can help in any way, please come and see me.'

The directrice sailed away and Megan popped Jantje into his cot. He was the last baby to be bathed, and it was time to start on the feeds, but first the older ones needed their mid-morning drinks. She had no time to think and that was a good thing; she had known that she would be leaving soon but now that it was a certainty she found herself unprepared for it.

She was off duty and at three o'clock she changed into a cotton dress and a cardigan and sandals and made for the beach. It had been a warm sultry morning, the sunshine hazy, and although the sky was blue there were clouds and a misty veil over it draining its colour. The sands stretched away on either side of her and she turned north towards Egmond-aan-Zee, four miles away. She had some money in her pocket and when she got tired she could turn into the dunes and take the path running parallel to the sea and find her way back on to the road and find a bus back to Castricum.

She walked steadily, deep in thought, making plans. She would go home, of course, but as soon as possible she would find a job, somewhere not too far from home yet far enough to avoid seeing Oscar more than occasionally. She had spent very little money in Holland and she had enough in the bank to tide her over the next few weeks; it only remained to decide exactly what sort of job she wanted. The obvious answer was surgery, she was well experienced in that, but she had enjoyed working with the babies; perhaps she could find something similar in England . . . She walked on, not noticing that the blue sky was now completely hidden and coming in from the sea at a great rate was a massive roll of black cloud.

The storm struck suddenly, a flash of lightning to strike her dumb, a crash of thunder to deafen her and then torrential rain. She stood for a moment, bemused, looking with dismay at the ugly clouds facing her racing nearer. At that she took to her heels and raced for the shelter of the dunes.

She was soaked before she reached the scanty shelter; it was difficult going through the fine sand and then the helm—the dune grass—and the shrubs and low-growing trees gave little protection, and all the time the lightning danced and sizzled around her and the thunder tumbled and crashed. Megan was a level-headed, sensible girl for the most part, but this sudden eruption of sound and fierce flashes was rather more than she liked and since no one could possibly hear her she allowed herself to scream; it relieved her feelings. She wiped her streaming face and cringed at another flash, thankful that there wasn't a really tall tree in sight. She dared to look over her shoulder and saw that the grey sky over the sea was a nasty black with a yellowish tinge; the storm was by no means lessening, and indeed there appeared to be worse to come. She worked her way deeper into the dunes, telling herself that if she kept going she would be bound to come to a road, but before long, what with the streaming rain, the noise and the lightning, augmented now by a fierce wind coming in from the sea, she lost her sense of direction, turning north instead of inland. The undergrowth was dense now and there were stunted trees and for a time the dunes hid the sea from her so that when she found herself on a sandy path she could have shouted with relief. Paths led somewhere, she reminded herself; the road couldn't be far off. The storm was at its height but she was past caring. She followed the path in the eerie half light, flinching at each flash and clap.

Presently she came to a fork in the path and after only a moment's pause took the right-hand one since the other would lead her back to the coast again—and plodded on, unaware that she was going further and further away from the orphanage with each step; quite disorientated, she imagined that she had the sea behind her and that she was going inland. She was numb with fright, soaked to the skin and possessed of only one thought—to reach the road as quickly as possible. The path ran straight ahead of her in the blinding rain, lighted every few moments by lightning flashes, one so shockingly vivid that she stood still stiff with fright, waiting for the explosion of thunder to follow, and it was then that she saw the patch of white at the side of the path. A plastic bag, one of millions that the countrywide supermarket Albert Heijn handed out to its customers. It had something in it, for she saw its faint movement and she picked it up gingerly and peered inside. The light was bad but not so bad that she was unable to see the baby wrapped in a piece of blanket inside it.

'Oh, my goodness me,' said Megan, for the moment impervious to lightning and thunder alike. 'You poor darling,' and she put an urgent and gentle hand inside the bag. The infant was alive. 'Thank heaven for that,' cried Megan. 'Now we find a road quickly...'

There had been an uncanny pause in the storm and she hurried along the path to be brought to a sudden breathless halt by the hail. It beat down on her like bullets from a gun and although she had the bag held close to her it beat down on the baby too. She did the only thing possible and crouched down in the undergrowth at the side of the path, cowering away from the renewed lightning and thunder claps, holding the baby against her. 'All I need,' said Megan in a loud voice to keep her spirits up, 'is a miracle.'

It wasn't until the evening meal that her friends at the orphanage started to worry about Megan. They had had a busy afternoon, dealing throughout with the childish terror caused by the storm, closing windows, and doors, and setting out candles and oil-lamps to light them when the electricity gave out.

'Which way did she go?' asked Anneke. 'Did anyone hear her say?'

No one had but one of the girls said, 'She told me last week that she was going to walk to Egmond-aan-Zee one day, but she didn't say when. Perhaps she went this afternoon...'

Someone told the directrice and while they were doing so the phone rang. It was Professor van Belfeld, wanting to know if they were all right at the orphanage.

'No electricity,' said the directrice, 'but we have candles and lamps. I am a little concerned about Megan—she went for a walk this afternoon and she isn't back. She may be sheltering somewhere, I'm told that she had mentioned that she wanted to take the path through the dunes to Egmond. Shall I let the police know?'

The professor's voice was quieter than ever. 'Not yet. I'm at home; I'll be over.'

So he was, within a very short time, throwing down his sopping Burberry and going at once to the direc-

trice's office, where they pored over the large map on
its wall. 'She was off duty at three o'clock? Allow half
an hour for changing her clothes...the storm struck at
half-past four more or less, which means she would have
been about three kilometres along the dune path—or the
beach. In any case she would have surely made for
shelter. Which means that she should be roughly here,
probably making for the coast road.' He pointed a long
finger at the map. 'I think it will be best if I take the
car along the road and go into the dunes from there. I
shall probably meet her.'

'You would like someone to go with you?'

'I think not. The weather is shocking outside, no need
to risk anyone else getting wet. I'd like a blanket if I
may...'

He got into his Burberry again, took the blanket and
went out into the violent weather and drove away down
the narrow road which ran behind the dunes.

He drove to the spot he had marked on the map,
switched on the car's lights, took his torch and got out.
The hail had stopped but the rain was still heavy as he
made his way towards the dunes, quite wide here and
heavily wooded at this point. The storm still raged but
the wind had died down so that between the thunder-
claps there was comparative silence except for the noise
of the incessant rain. As he reached the dunes he paused
to find a path before plunging into the undergrowth,
stopping every now and then to shout. For such a quiet
man he had a formidable voice but there was no reply
as he went deeper towards the sea, lighted at one moment
by the lightning and the next plunged into darkness with
only his torch to guide him. It was between two thun-
derclaps that he at last heard a voice answer his shout.
He had stopped where two paths crossed each other, and

stumbling towards him was Megan, a deplorable sight, wringing wet, her hair plastered on her head and clutching the plastic bag.

For such a powerfully built man, he moved with incredible speed. She felt his arms around her and burst into tears, so that whatever it was that the professor said in his own language escaped her. She drew a snivelling breath. 'Jake, oh, Jake.' She peered up at his calm face. 'There's a baby in the bag.'

CHAPTER NINE

THE professor took Megan's news with commendable lack of surprise. He took the carrier-bag from her and shone his torch upon the sleeping infant inside it. He asked no tiresome questions, merely dropped a kiss on to her wet cheek, tucked the bag under one arm and urged her gently back along the path he had taken.

She was tired and wet and frightened but somehow none of that seemed to matter any more. She was scarcely aware of being led back to the car, scooped up into the blanketed front seat, the baby in the plastic bag once more on her lap and the short journey back to the orphanage under way. Once there she was bustled inside, aware of the professor giving instructions in an unhurried voice before she was hurried away to be undressed, stood under a hot shower until she glowed and then popped into bed. It was Anneke who did this, presently joined by Sine with a mug of hot milk, both of them uttering soothing remarks.

'Oh, is the directrice very angry?' asked Megan, sitting up in bed, a normal colour once again and blissfully warm.

'Angry? Why should she be angry?' asked Sine. 'She is only happy that you are safe. It is a very bad storm with much damage and accidents, and besides you have saved a baby's life.'

'A boy or a girl? I—I couldn't see very well.'

'A girl—newly born. The professor and Dr Timuss are with her now.'

Megan sipped her milk and presently the directrice arrived to see her.

'A bad experience for you, Megan,' she observed kindly. 'Most happily you were found by the professor. It is to be hoped that you have come to no harm.'

'I feel quite well, thank you, Directrice,' said Megan politely. 'Is the baby all right?'

'It is a mercy that you found her and kept her safe. She will need care—she is, the professor thinks, only a day or so old—but babies are tough. She is to be called Megan and when she is old enough we shall tell her that she owes her life to you.' She broke off as there was a knock on the door and the professor came in. He ranged himself beside the directrice, staring down at Megan, who was, in fact, quite worth staring at; she had a healthy pink colour now and her hair, washed and dried, hung in a dark cloud around her shoulders and her nightie, pink and lace-trimmed, revealed a good deal of her charming person. The directrice, whose own nightwear was both concealing and sensible, gave a little cough; the professor transferred his gaze to the wallpaper and Megan, innocent of the effect she was having, looked at her enquiringly.

'Professor van Belfeld wishes to make sure that you have come to no harm. Megan, you feel well?'

Megan assured her for the second time that she felt very well.

The professor lowered his eyes from the wallpaper. 'You are a strong and healthy girl, and you should come to no harm, but if you have a sore throat or feel unwell perhaps you will let the directrice know at once.' He smiled in a wintry way. 'We must send you back to England perfectly fit.'

Megan agreed bleakly and then, anxious to appear eager to return home, said brightly, 'Oh, yes, I'm so looking forward to that. I've loved being here but it's time I went back to a hospital—I shall miss the children and the other girls, they've been so friendly...' She stopped, aware that she was babbling, and the professor was eyeing her with a faint lift of the eyebrows and a nasty curl of the lip.

Then he turned away, saying, 'I'm glad that you have come to no harm. The baby is, against all odds, in good shape. I'm taking her with me now to Leiden; she will be in Intensive Care for a while but as soon as she is big and strong enough she will come here.' He held the door open for the directrice. 'Goodnight, Megan,' he said.

'Goodnight, sir; goodnight, Directrice.' She threw a pillow at the closed door by way of relieving her feelings and then allowed herself the comfort of a quiet weep. She felt better then and when Sine came in with supper on a tray—an unwonted luxury—she was sitting up in bed with a newly washed face which, though pale, gave no sign of tears. Lying in bed presently her thoughts were of the professor; she was never going to understand him; when he had found her on the dunes he had held her close and although she hadn't understood what he had said it had sounded loving; besides she had had a glimpse of his face... but just now, when he had come to see her with the directrice, he had been coolly impersonal, as though they had never shared those few minutes in the storm. She went to sleep presently, and, waking early, was glad that she was on duty at seven o'clock.

There was a letter for her in the morning; the professor's grandmother, having heard that she would be going back to England very shortly, would like her to go and bid her goodbye and would she care to go to lunch on her next free day? The note was written in a beautiful spidery hand and requested an answer as soon as possible, adding that a car would be sent to call for her.

Megan still hadn't been told exactly when she was leaving; she wrote back at once saying that she had a day off in two days' time and would very much like to see Mevrouw van Belfeld.

The orphanage had settled down again into its quiet routine, and the weather, after the freak storm, had settled down too to a mild warmth with a good deal of sunshine; the place rang with the sound of children's voices, and Dr Timuss, paying his usual visit, remarked that it was a pity that Megan would be leaving just when there seemed the prospect of a fine summer.

'Little Megan is thriving,' he told her. 'She is out of Intensive Care and gaining weight. The police are trying to trace her mother but there isn't much hope of that. If no one claims her she will come here in a few weeks— the storm must have been pretty frightening. A good thing that Professor van Belfeld phoned the directrice when he did. He worked out where you would be and found you almost at once, didn't he? Never at a loss even in a dire emergency. He's going back to England very shortly, I hear. Any idea when you're leaving?'

'None; I expect it depends on Mien coming back from Canada. It doesn't really matter to me, for I shall be going home for a bit.'

He picked up Lise's chart and studied her weight. 'Well, send a postcard, won't you? We shall all miss you.'

'I shall miss everyone here—I've been very happy...'

'You weren't happy when you came, were you?'

'No.' She smiled at him. 'There's nothing like a pack of infants and children to take one's mind off oneself.'

She dressed carefully for her visit to Baroness van Belfeld; a pretty dress in muted pinks and blues in a fine voile with a simple bodice, short sleeves and a wide, softly pleated skirt. She was to be fetched at half-past eleven and she went down to the hall with a minute or two to spare, stopping on the way to tell Annette where she was going.

'Not Mevrouw,' said Annette severely. 'You must say Baroness.'

'Oh, must I? I hope I haven't been impolite...'

'No, no. She will be glad to see you, I think. Now that Professor van Belfeld has gone to England she will be lonely.'

'Gone to England? Oh...' Megan added a quick, 'Yes, of course.'

As she went out of the door she admitted to herself that she had hoped to see the professor; that he might perhaps fetch her in his car. There was a car there, but not his, of course. A beautifully kept and rather out of date Daimler with a youngish man waiting by it.

He opened the door for her, bade her, '*Goeden dag*,' and added, 'I am son of Litman, Dirk.'

Megan got in beside him. 'You speak English, how nice. I can't speak Dutch, only a few words.'

'Very difficult.' He was a friendly man and they talked about this and that as he drove, using a mixture of both languages and rather enjoying themselves. Megan would have liked to have asked him about the professor but she wouldn't stoop to that; perhaps his grandmother would tell her if he had gone for good or if he would return. She would be leaving very soon now, within a week perhaps; it depended on a final letter from Mien as to the exact date. She did her best to stop thinking about him and when they reached the house she thanked Dirk and was led by a dignified but welcoming Litman to a small sitting-room where the baroness was waiting.

The welcome from the old lady was warm. 'How pretty you look, child,' she observed. 'Jake told me that you were twenty-eight but you look ten years younger. You look so much better since you have been at the orphanage. The good sea air and the simple food have done wonders.'

Megan sat down near her. 'The children too,' she pointed out. 'I've loved every minute of it.'

They drank their coffee from delicate porcelain cups and ate small crisp biscuits and talked about clothes and old furniture and the portraits on the walls and not a word about the professor. It was most frustrating. Megan bent to stroke the ginger cat curled up on the silk Kashan rug and asked with sudden inspiration, 'Does she get on well with the dogs?'

'Indeed yes, yes, she misses them when they aren't here. They are out walking with the gardener's boy— they in their turn miss Jake. I miss him too, just as I shall miss everything here when I go back to den Haag.'

'Oh, I thought you lived here...'

The old lady shook her head. 'I have my own apartments in the house of my son and his wife—Jake's parents. They are in New Zealand visiting his sister, who is married to a surgeon in Wellington. They return shortly and I shall go back with them.' She studied Megan's questioning face. 'You wonder why they do not live here in this large house? They have a patrician house in den Haag. It has been in the family for a long time, just as this one—Jake is the eldest son and it has been the custom in the family for the eldest son, when he becomes twenty-one years of age, to live here, marry and bring up his family and when the time comes his son will take over this house and he in his turn will go to den Haag.'

Well, thought Megan, I've known the professor all these months without discovering anything about him and now his granny has said a good deal of it in one sentence. She said politely, 'How interesting. Only the professor isn't married...'

His grandmother peered at her over her spectacles. 'Not yet. The van Belfeld men have never hurried to marry but when they finally do so it is for life and beyond, and they marry for love and for no other reason. Jake has said nothing to me but I feel that you have been unhappy—still are. You are perhaps in love? Would you like to talk about it? It does help...'

Megan said, 'It's such a dull little story; I think it must happen all the time. I was engaged to someone, I thought that I loved him and that he loved me—we got on well together and liked each other's company—but I know now that I didn't love him, only you see I didn't know that then because I had never been in love. It's quite different, isn't it,' she looked at her companion, 'being in love, loving someone so that nothing else matters? He—he met my sister, who's a darling girl, and they fell in love just like that—so I had to do something about it.' She hesitated. 'Professor van Belfeld helped me—he found me a job so that I could get away and when I got here and could see everything from a distance I could see how different it was. So now I'm all right again.'

'And none the worse for it,' observed the baroness briskly, 'but tell me, why are you sad—there is something—someone else?'

It was tempting to confide in her companion but Megan stopped just in time. Her denial was so vigorous that she very nearly believed it herself.

Even if the old lady hadn't had a pretty good idea of the situation, Megan gave herself away by asking in an over-casual manner, 'Has the professor gone back to England?'

'Yes, unexpectedly. Some urgent matter and it seems that he is expert in whatever it is and no one else would do. They would like him to take a post in the United States—a very tempting offer.'

'Oh, no.' Megan had uttered it so fiercely that she tried at once to make it sound different. 'What I mean is, he would be missed here and in London too, wouldn't he?'

'Indeed. Fortunately, he has no need to consider financial gain, as he has a sufficient income. Now, do tell me something of your plans, Megan.'

Megan would have liked to have gone on talking about the professor but her companion had spoken briskly, shutting the door on the topic of her grandson.

'Well, they are rather vague at the moment. I'm not quite sure when I'm leaving the orphanage although it will be very soon, I think. I shall go home for a little while...'

'You don't mean to return to Regent's Hospital?'

'No, oh, no. I'd like to go right away. Scotland perhaps. I—I haven't decided yet.'

The baroness began to talk about the storm and the damage it had done and presently Litman came in with a tray of sherry, and, after a suitable interval, announced lunch.

They went to the dining-room, the baroness holding on to Megan's arm and using a stick and at the same time contriving to walk with dignity, and they lunched off cold lettuce soup, chicken breasts in a delicate cheese sauce, accompanied by a green salad and followed by strawberry tarts.

'We will have coffee in the drawing-room,' observed the baroness, 'and then you shall have a pleasant walk in the gardens while I take my nap.'

So Megan found herself wandering among the flowerbeds and presently found her way to the kitchen garden, exquisitely laid out in neat rows of peas and beans, lettuce and spinach, onions and carrots, its red-brick walls clad with espaliered fruit trees. There was an arched wooden door in the wall, and she opened it and peered through. Beyond there was a paddock and then water meadows and a glimpse of water in the distance. Lovely for the dogs, she thought, and saw them, racing to meet her with Litman's son behind them. It was hardly a race; Swift had reached her long before Rosie lolloped up to join them.

When Dirk reached her, Megan asked, 'Is this also belonging to the—the baron?'

Dirk waved an arm. 'To the water—he has much land.'

They walked back to the house together, the dogs running to and fro until they parted, Dirk to take the dogs through the kitchen door and she to go quietly through the french window into the drawing-room where she had left the old lady resting on one of the sofas.

The baroness had wakened, and, much refreshed, embarked on a rambling history of the house and gardens. Megan listened avidly, for anything to do with the professor compelled her full attention. The old lady was only brought to a halt by the arrival of the tea tray.

'A pleasant English habit,' remarked the old lady happily. 'Assam tea which Jake has sent from Fortnum and Mason, made in the English manner with milk.'

Megan sat for another half-hour before suggesting that it was time for her to leave, and once again the car was brought round to the front door and she was ushered into it by Dirk. The baroness wished her goodbye cheerfully enough and offered an elderly cheek for her kiss. 'I am quite sure you have a very happy future, my dear,' she said as they parted.

The next day the directrice sent for Megan; Mien would be back in two days' time and Megan would be free to leave. 'I would be grateful if you could remain with us for one more day,' said the directrice, 'so that you may hand over to Mien. You are on the afternoon shift, are you not? Will you come on duty as usual tomorrow and on the following day take the seven o'clock duty? Mien will be with us late tomorrow evening so that you can work together until noon. That will give you ample time to get to Amsterdam and catch the evening boat train for the Hoek. You will return by boat?'

They had discussed her departure on several occasions and Megan had told the directrice that she would prefer to go back by the night ferry.

'Very well, you may make your arrangements now if you wish while you have help in the nursery. Let me know if there is anything I can do or if you cannot get a reservation. You know that you are welcome to stay if necessary until there is a free berth.'

There was a berth; Megan checked the trains and the time of the night sailing and then went back to the nursery. She would phone her mother in the morning and pack then, her mind busy with all the small chores to be done before she left. She should be feeling happy at the idea of going home, she reflected, but all she could think of was the fact that she wasn't going to see the professor again.

The next day she was walking up and down the balcony with a peevish Jantje cradled in her arms when the professor trod silently into the nursery and fetched up beside her.

Megan, conscious of a wild delight at the sight of him, said in a small voice, 'Oh, I thought you were in England.'

'I am just this morning returned from there.'

'Oh—oh, well. I'm glad you came. I'm going home tomorrow. I thought I wouldn't see you again—I was going to write...'

'What about?' His voice was quiet yet compelling.

'To thank you. You were right, I did need to go away—and look at everything from a distance. I had no idea...I didn't know what being in love—loving someone—was, did I? It isn't enough just to be fond of someone and enjoy their company, it's your whole life...'

'And you have discovered that, Megan?' He spoke softly and she responded, forgetting caution.

'Yes.' She looked into his calm face. 'I shan't see you again, shall I? I'm going to take a job as far away from London as possible. Besides, someone told me that you were planning to live more here than in London.' When he nodded she went on, 'Perhaps you won't want to know this but I think I owe it to you: you see I discovered that I had never been in love with Oscar because I'm in love with you. I didn't know that, of course; I liked you and I trusted you, but it wasn't until you brought me here and left me without saying anything that I discovered that it was you.' She paused. 'I watched the back of you walking away and I felt—I don't think there's a word.'

Her eyes were on his face. 'That's all I wanted to say,' she said baldly. 'I hope you aren't...' She was interrupted by two things: Dr Timuss advancing towards them and the look of concentration on Jantje's face, slowly crimsoning with effort. 'Oh, the lamb, he needs changing.' She bore him away and the professor gave a crack of laughter as he turned to greet the other man. When Megan got back into the nursery both men had gone and when she went down for her tea break and peered out of the window there was no sign of the professor's car.

She gave a great sigh of relief, red in the face at the memory of the things she had said to him. She must have been mad, she reflected; she hadn't meant to have said what she had, only somehow he was a man she could confide in and once she had started it had been impossible to stop.

She met Mien that evening when she at last got off duty. A stout, round-faced girl with pale hair and a pair of bright blue eyes. Her English was good and she had a great deal to say about Canada. 'All the same,' she declared, 'it is nice to be back here. You are sorry to go, Megan?'

'Yes!' said Megan. 'I've enjoyed every minute, only I must get back and find a job in England.'

They met again at seven o'clock the next morning and spent several hours working together until it was time for Megan to say goodbye to the babies and Mien and eat a hasty lunch before getting out of her overall for the last time and dressing in the little grey jacket and its matching skirt. The day was overcast and probably it would be raining in England. She went around saying goodbye to everyone, ending with the directrice, and everyone crowded to the door to see her off. A car would take her to Castricum station, the directrice had told her, and there was a general chorus of well wishers as she went outside.

The Rolls-Royce was there with the professor leaning against it. He had nothing to say, and, without giving her time to utter, he opened the door and popped her into the front seat, put her case in the boot and got in beside her.

'There's a car,' began Megan faintly. 'I'm catching a train at Castricum,' and when he took no notice at all she said, 'I'm going to England,' with something of a snap.

'All in good time.' He waved to the group standing in the entrance and she waved and smiled too, feeling as though she had been hit on the head.

'Are you going to England?' she asked urgently as he drove out on to the road.

'Yes,' and when she began, 'But why...?' he said, 'Hush, later.'

She hushed for all of a minute and then said, 'I don't know what you are doing or why. I shall miss my train.'

When he didn't reply she asked, 'Are we going all the way to the Hoek?'

'No.'

She sat up very straight. 'If it's because of what I said yesterday then please forget it. I—I was a bit upset.'

'You didn't mean a word of it?' She remained silent and he said softly, 'Answer me, Megan.'

She turned a shoulder to him, looking unseeingly out of the window. 'Of course I meant it,' she mumbled. 'Where are we going?' she asked presently in a small voice.

'Home.'

He wasn't going to tell her anything; she sat silently exploring all the reasons for his strange behaviour. Perhaps he had another job for her? Or his granny might have expressed a wish to see her again, in which case she would certainly miss her train and the ferry as well. Perhaps he just wanted to give her a lecture on the lack of wisdom in letting her feelings take over from common sense and decent pride. It would be, she decided, the last.

'You haven't any right,' she began, speaking her thoughts out loud, to be silenced by his,

'Oh, yes, I have, and here we are.'

She got out of the car silently when he opened the door and stood uncertainly. There was no sign of Litman; the house door remained closed as the professor propelled her briskly across the lawn, down the path to the kitchen garden through the little wooden door to the paddock beyond.

'Why?' began Megan, quite bewildered.

'Because we are quite alone here, my darling, and I have no wish to propose to you with an audience, however discreet, breathing down our necks. I was beginning to think that you would never discover that you loved me. I have been very patient, have I not? Waiting for you to get over Oscar and then waiting for you to fall in love with me. I am a patient man, dear love, but I have loved you for a while now, indeed I fell in love with you the first time I set eyes on you months ago. I have been sorely tempted to tell you at times, but you needed time, and after all we shall have the rest of our lives together.'

He gathered her close and kissed her. For a professor of pathology, thought Megan dreamily, he kissed very nicely. When she had her breath again she said, 'I should like to know——'

'Yes, yes, my darling, I'm sure you would, but first, will you marry me?'

'Yes, oh, yes, Jake, but I should like to know——'

'Don't waste time asking silly questions, my love.' So she didn't, but presently she pulled a little away from him. 'I've missed my train,' she told him.

'You're staying here tonight. My mother and father are back from New Zealand and waiting here to meet you.' He kissed the tip of her nose. 'How delightfully pretty you are. We'll go and meet them. I phoned your mother this afternoon.'

'Do you mean to say you told Mother that I wasn't coming home tomorrow? How did you know that? Supposing I had refused to come with you this afternoon? What would you have done?'

The professor thought for a moment. 'Followed you to the station and abducted you.'

Her eyes shone. 'Really?'

'Really. You see, my dearest girl, I love you.'

'Oh, Jake, I want to stay with you forever.' She looked up at him with such a loving face that he bent to kiss it just once more.

'I shall take care that you do,' he told her, 'and now let us go home.'